I0700602

Cutler's Friend

a John Cutler mystery

by Colin Conway

Sticks and stones may break my bones,
but words will never hurt me

\- children's taunt

Cutler's Friend

2006

Chapter 1

Even though it was a wig, the long blond hair looked natural. It cascaded beyond her left clavicle yet did nothing to disguise the breadth of her shoulders. The length of the purple dress was below her knees. The fabric seemed airy and light—perfect for a summer evening. Perhaps, it clung a little too tight to her midsection, but it was still a nice choice.

She strolled by the restaurant's windows but didn't bother to look in. Maybe it was confidence. Perhaps it was because she had no idea what I looked like and gawking for me would call further attention to herself. Had she looked, though, I might have waved—probably *would* have waved. Regardless, she flowed by the window—a big woman on a mission.

I'd already waited twenty minutes for Terry Newsome to arrive. Better to be early than arrive tardy and discover that she left upon not finding me. The meeting was my request and expected to take only a few minutes. Therefore, it was my burden to be there first, even if that meant some missed time with my visiting daughter.

This was Erin's final day in town. We spent most of it together in Riverfront Park. Above everything, she wanted to ride the Looff Carrousel once more before leaving. It seemed a funny request from a newly minted teenager, but I agreed to do it again—anything to keep the little girl in her alive a while longer. Tomorrow morning, she would head home to the west side of the state and her mother. It was surprising how fast a week went by.

After stepping inside, Terry Newsome clutched a small purse and searched the lobby. Not seeing me there, her eyes went deeper into the restaurant until she saw my raised hand.

As she strode in my direction, I noticed her heels. They were light purple and matched the dress. They weren't too high but tall enough for me to appreciate. It made it tough to gauge her height but not her poise. Terry was a graceful woman.

She stopped next to the table. "Mr. Cutler?"

I nodded. "Call me John."

Tucking her dress behind her knees, she slid into the booth. She set her purse on the seat next to her. "Thank you."

"For?"

"Being polite." Her eyes flicked briefly toward the bar.

It was then I noticed it. The high rumble of chatter that had been in the restaurant before Terry's entrance was now a low hum of rumor and innuendo. Many heads turned in our direction.

"We can go elsewhere," I said. "Some place more discreet."

She waved a dismissive hand. "It's the same wherever. Nothing changes."

I didn't know what to say, so I remained quiet. I'd already made peace with my biases. Terry Newsome was born differently than she dressed. It was something I couldn't quite comprehend. Maybe it made her feel good. Perhaps she was searching for something. My job wasn't to criticize her choices. It was to get something back.

A server in her mid-twenties walked over and opened her notepad. She cast a bored glance to Terry then eyed me with equal apathy. "Can I get you two something?" She'd probably worked a downtown restaurant long enough to see this type of scene before.

Terry's eyes shifted to the server. "Just a water, please. No ice. With a slice of lemon."

"You?" she asked me. "Ready now?"

"A cup of decaf. Black."

"Anything else?"

I shook my head.

She frowned and walked off.

"A couple of big spenders," Terry said.

The bar must have gotten bored with Terry's presence because the roar of after-work excitement returned. Behind me, a table full of fraternity rejects cheered something occurring on a television.

I leaned in. "Where's it at?"

Terry sighed. "Why won't she talk with me?"

"That's not my concern. Marian hired me to get the ring back."

"A private investigator." She frowned and turned to look through the window. Or maybe she was checking out her reflection. Whatever she was doing was wasting time I could potentially spend with my daughter.

"Please, Terry. I need the ring. She's prepared to pay for it."

Her face contorted, but she continued to look out the window. "You think I did it for money?"

"I don't know why you did it."

Looking at me now, she said, "I want her to talk with me."

"She's not going to. That's why she got the no-contact order."

"I didn't do anything to deserve that."

"The court thinks differently. Then you went and

proved them right by taking the ring."

"But she's avoiding me."

I stared at her.

"Why won't she talk with me?" Terry whined.

"I'm not a counselor. Where's the ring?"

She shrugged.

"Let's not play this game. You took it to hurt her."

Terry held a hand to her chest and feigned shock.

"We both know it worked. Now, give it back."

Her features hardened. "Not until she talks with me."

"The no-contact order," I reminded her.

"Totally bogus."

"You didn't leave harassing phone calls at her work?"

She rolled her eyes. "Okay, maybe I shouldn't have done that, but I was upset." She tapped the table. "Why is she the only one who gets to be upset? She broke it off. I'm hurt, too."

"That's old news."

"Not to me."

"We're not going to change it tonight."

Terry looked away—this time into the bar. She must have seen something she didn't like because she turned back. "Some people," she muttered.

"Where's it at, Terry? Where's the ring?"

"I don't know."

Terry leaned back from the table as the server returned. The younger woman placed a glass of water in front of Terry and a white ceramic mug in front of me. She also set a small container of sugar and powdered milk packets on the table. "Change your mind on something to eat?"

I shook my head.

"Maybe later," Terry offered cheerfully.

The server nodded politely and walked away.

"Nice girl," Terry said.

"The ring. For the third time, where is it?"

She pulled her glass to her and lifted the lemon slice from the water. With manicured fingers, Terry squeezed it. "For the third time—I do not know."

"You were the only one who knew where it was, the only one who knows how much that ring meant, and the only one who knew how to get into Marian's house without a key."

"*Please*." She bit into the fruit slice and puckered. Her face scrunched, and she playfully shook her head. The long hair flopped away from her left shoulder. When she regained her composure, Terry pulled the hair back to where it was previously. "When she got the ring, Marian showed it to all our friends. Told everyone how it had been her mother's. How her father had scrimped and saved to buy it, then proposed on his knee up at Cliff Park. Blah blah blah. Oh, my God, she loves that story. Everyone knew what it meant and where she kept it. Somebody else has it."

"No one else took it. You did."

Terry looked at the window again. This time I was sure she was considering her reflection since she briefly made duck lips. "After her mother died…" Terry let the words hang in the air for so long that I thought she lost her train of thought. She inhaled deeply and held it. Then she said, "Marian changed. She wasn't the woman I got involved with anymore."

It was the pot calling the kettle black, and I'd had enough. This should have been a simple handoff, but Terry was making it a bigger show than it needed to be. And, because of that, I was missing time with Erin. The whole thing pissed me off.

"So, what if she changed? I'm sure the same thing could be said of you, *Terrance*."

She slowly turned to me as her eyes narrowed.

I'd gone too far, and I knew it. As a private investigator, dealing with people is often an artform—one that I'm not always proficient in. It's especially tough when I'm battling my own prejudices. There's an old saying about catching more flies with honey, but I'm just as likely to bring a pile of feces to capture those same flies.

"I'm sorry," I said.

"Neanderthal."

I raised a hand in deference. "I am sorry."

She grabbed her purse and glared at me.

"Listen," I said, "Marian hasn't reported the ring stolen. She doesn't want you in any more trouble. She just wants it back."

Terry's jaw tightened, and her eyes bore into me. "Pay the tab."

"Huh?"

"The ring is in my car." She slid out of the booth and slung the purse over her shoulder.

"For real?"

"The sooner I give it back, the sooner I can be away from you and done with this whole mess."

I laid a ten-dollar bill on the table and stood.

Terry led the way out of the restaurant. On the heels, she stood a couple of inches taller than me. Even from this view, I was still impressed by her dexterity in the shoes.

Once outside, she stopped on the sidewalk and stared up at the Claremont Apartments where I had previously lived. "How many stories are in this city?"

"I don't know what you're talking about."

"That old television show," Terry said. "Eight million

stories in the city. How many are in this one? Two hundred thousand?" She faced me. "Well, this is my story." She grabbed her dress and splayed it out. "Marian knew this is who I was. Who I am. I didn't keep anything secret."

I don't know when Marian learned about the dresses, but she seemed okay with it. She explained that when Terrance got made up like this, he desired to be called a woman and referred to with feminine labels. Marian might not have fully grasped what Terrance felt, but she used terms like gender fluidity and dysphoria to describe what he was going through.

Tears welled in Terry's eyes. "I never would have thought it would come to this. Her sending a goon after me."

"Aw, hell, Terry. You took the ring, and I'm no goon."

She wiped away some tears and smeared her mascara. "You're bought and paid for. That's the definition of a goon."

Through the bank of windows lining the restaurant, several patrons watched us. A table full of men laughed at Terry. Maybe they were laughing at me, too. I don't know. Seeing their intolerance so blatantly on display made me ashamed of my own. I scowled at them, but that seemed to make them laugh harder.

"Do you think you can stop me?" Tears rolled down her cheeks.

"What?"

Terry angrily wiped her chin. "I'm not giving it to you. Not now."

"What did I do?"

Inside the bar, the guys at the window howled with delight. One of them jumped and pointed. It seemed others were crowding around their table to get an eyeful of the big woman as she melted down.

Terry must have caught their motion from the corner of her eye because she turned to watch them. She pulled her shoulders back, set her jaw, and took a deep breath. "I want to talk with her. Not you."

"But you can't."

Once more, Terry faced me. "You're not going to tell me what I can and can't do." She lifted the palm of her hand and held it in front of my face. "I'm done."

She turned to leave, but I grabbed her wrist.

Shocked, Terry said, "Let go."

"*Wait.*"

She tried to yank free, but I held tight.

"Get your hand off me."

"Not until you give me the ring."

Anger flared in her eyes. "I'll cry rape."

I barked a single laugh. "Get real. Nobody's gonna believe—"

With her free hand, she slapped my face.

I should have prepared for it. My laugh was disrespectful, and this moment was already charged enough. It wasn't the first time a woman had slapped me, but it was the first time it had the power of a large man behind it. I spun, my knees buckled, and I fell into a window.

The group inside the restaurant cheered with delight. This is what it must feel like to be on the other side of the glass in a hockey rink.

When I righted myself, Terry was already moving down the sidewalk. Damn, she flowed in those heels. She crossed the street and was into the neighboring parking lot before I made it to her.

"Terry," I hollered. "Wait."

She stopped digging in her purse. "Stay away from me. I'm warning you."

"The ring." I held out my hand. "Maybe Marian will talk after she has it back."

"You're trying to trick me."

"I just want the ring."

"Walk away now. You don't want this fight."

"I don't want to hit a woman." I felt stupid for saying that, but I was trying—really trying—to be respectful.

She set her purse on the hood of her car and lifted her hands. "This will go badly for you."

I smiled. "Terry, I think you have me confused with someone else. You're not going to surprise me again."

A crowd from the bar formed on the opposite corner. Several of them chanted, "Fight! Fight!" while the rest hooted with derisive laughter.

Terry shifted her weight onto the balls of her feet. She looked like a fighter preparing for the bell to start a round. It was odd to see a woman in a dress and heels assume that posture.

I spread my hands wide and affected a disarming smile. "C'mon, man, are we really going to do this?"

"*Man?*"

She jabbed. It was so fast and straight that I hadn't seen it coming until it hit me in the face. I stumbled back a couple of feet. Terry moved forward. The grace she had shown before was nothing like she displayed now. She was crouched and on the balls of her feet—the heels were off the ground.

Across the street, the assembled mob roared with laughter. "Bitch blasted you good!" someone yelled.

I lifted my hands to a guard position and blinked the tears from my eyes.

"I was a Golden Gloves champion," Terry said. "Treat me with some respect."

"I'm trying, man. All I want—"

"*Man?*"

She fired another jab—a beautiful stiff one. But I spotted it and rolled under it. The pride I felt in my evasive move was short-lived as I realized too late that the punch was only a decoy. It moved me to where she wanted—bent over and looking up. A right cross clicked across my chin, and I dropped to the ground.

The crowd danced and cheered with delight.

"Stay down," Terry said. "You're no match."

I lifted a hand in surrender. She was right. Even in heels, she was right. Humiliated, I rolled to my butt and touched my jaw.

Terry walked to her car and picked up her purse. It only took a moment to find her keys.

"Hey," I said.

She opened the driver's door.

"Give me the ring."

"Like hell."

"Or I'm gonna call the cops."

Terry paused as she had started to climb in. "So?"

Shakily, I stood. The second punch was a hell of a shot.

"What are you going to tell them?" she asked. "That you accosted me?"

"Is that what the witnesses will say?"

She looked over my shoulder to the still-hooting crowd.

"You think I'm embarrassed to say I got beat up by a woman?" I was, but the whole bar saw. It was too late for my pride now.

Terry's gaze returned to me.

"And when I tell them you're a Golden Gloves

champion, well, that's going to look pretty bad. I mean, I had no chance, right? You even said so."

Her face slackened when I reached into my pocket and pulled out my flip phone.

"What are you doing?" she asked.

"Calling the cops like I said."

She lifted a hand. "Wait."

"And when I tell them you stole Marian's ring, she can get it back that way. I mean, she didn't want to involve the cops, but she didn't say anything about me not calling them. I don't know why I didn't think of this sooner. Would have saved a lot of embarrassment."

"Wait a goddamned minute!"

I lowered the phone.

She pointed into her car. "It's in the console."

Terry bent inside. When she stepped back out, she tossed a little box. Inside was a simple diamond ring. It hardly seemed worth the fuss, but most family heirlooms weren't. I snapped the box closed.

Terry said, "I only wanted her to know how much she hurt me."

"She knows."

"She changed the locks before she told me we were over. Who does that?"

I started to turn.

"Tell her that I love her."

"She knows," I called over my shoulder.

"I'll always love her," he yelled.

"She probably knows that, too."

I was halfway to the laughing crowd when I thought better of it. Turning south, I headed into the alley. It was the long way back to my truck but screw it. My ego was bruised enough. I didn't need to go through a bunch of jackals just to show that their words wouldn't hurt me.

Chapter 2

The following day Erin sat next to me and quietly picked at a loose thread on her backpack. We were waiting for a Seattle boarding announcement. The blue plastic bench we sat upon was uncomfortable and covered in graffiti scratches.

People scurried throughout the station, hurrying for the arrivals and departures of both Greyhound buses and Amtrak trains.

It was Tuesday morning. Four days remained until the beginning of Hoopfest, Spokane's annual three-on-three basketball tournament. Every year, tourists piled into the city, booked up every available hotel room, and turned the ordinarily laid-back town into a giant hassle. Watching people enter the lobby from an arriving bus, it seemed that the yearly pilgrimage had started early. Several groups of young men carried basketballs under their arms.

Television monitors were hung around the lobby and played shows without sound. A soap opera ran on one screen. Cable news was on another. A third displayed a shopping network. It seemed most folks, even the men, were drawn to the image of a woman demonstrating the effectiveness of a pair of stretchy leggings. The model in the stockings could have been a *Playboy* centerfold. I'm sure most men watching didn't care about the discount if they ordered a pair now.

Erin didn't notice any of the televisions, though. She continued to tug on the backpack's string. "I'm glad I got to spend some time with you."

"Me, too," I said.

Teenage girls aren't impressed by cosmetic subtlety. Erin was no different. It seemed she applied everything with a heavy hand. Her eyes appeared almost sunken due to combined liner, shadow, and mascara. The blush on her cheeks pushed her bones higher than they were, and the lipstick made her lips fuller. She hadn't arrived wearing any of it but plastered it on the first morning here. I complained, which upset her. My girlfriend stepped in and convinced me to ease off.

"She's experimenting," Erika had said. "And her mom won't let her do it at home."

"You don't wear that stuff."

Erika smiled knowingly. "I went through that phase. Same as most. She'll get over it."

Watching my daughter play with her backpack, I asked, "Will your mom be okay with you wearing that make-up?"

Erin stifled a laugh. "Are you kidding? She'll have a cow."

"Are you going to take it off?"

"I haven't decided yet."

"How will you do it on the bus?"

Erin opened the backpack and removed a plastic baggie. Inside was a wetted washcloth. "Erika did this for me. She also gave me a packet of wet wipes and some paper towels." The corners of her eyes crinkled when she smiled. "She's so cool."

"Yeah. She's that."

"I like her, Dad."

"I'm glad you guys got a chance to hang out."

A voice boomed over the speaker that boarding for Seattle would begin in a few minutes. I disliked sending her home on a bus. Her mother and I had previously met in Ellensburg when I picked her up, but Erin wanted to ride a Greyhound home. I offered to travel with her, but she said she wanted to do it alone. Now that she was thirteen, she could do such a thing.

She explained she wanted a solo experience, so she could see new things and spread her wings. It would help her artistic creativity, she added. After a bunch of begging that was meant to be convincing, we relented. Of course, that was after we checked into the bus's security features and how they would monitor her. Her mother would still meet her in Ellensburg—that was the compromise we made. She agreed, of course, since we gave her no other option.

Upon arriving at that station, I completed the Unaccompanied Child form with her mother's and my contact info.

"This is going to be cool," Erin said.

"Yeah."

She laughed. "OMG, Dad. Relax."

My brow furrowed. "What did you say?"

"It's keyboard slang for oh, my God. We do it on MySpace."

"What the hell is MySpace?"

Erin rolled her eyes. I'd gotten that response a lot this week. "It's online. Erika joined my Friend Space this week. Now, we'll be able to talk any time." She grabbed my arm. "You could do it, too."

"I *could*. Why don't you like talking with me on the phone?"

Another eye roll. "I like talking to you." She didn't sound convincing.

"But you like this online thing better."

She shrugged. "It's what we do."

"Right."

Erin turned her attention back to the bus. "This ride is going to be cool."

I was counting cools now. She was up to three since we'd arrived which was fine. It was a word I liked and used myself. It was better than a slew of other choices—things she could be learning in places like MySpace.

"Maybe I'll even get a short story out of it," Erin said.

"Out of MySpace?"

She scrunched her face. "What? No." She pointed toward the bus.

"Oh, sure. Listen, you're already an artist." I tapped her backpack. She'd drawn in a sketchbook daily, and she journaled most mornings. "You finished that picture while you were here. I could never do something like that."

She slung the backpack over her shoulder. "You're so weird. I'll be an artist when something gets published." She eyed me with earnestness. "Until then, I'm just a nerd with a journal. Nobody cares."

"Don't forget the sketchpad."

Another eye roll. I should have been counting those along with the cools.

Erin said, "I'm not going to draw superheroes for a living. That's for fun."

She headed for the line forming outside. I had to hurry to keep up with her. Compared to my trepidation about this moment, she seemed fearless. She must have sensed my worry because she squeezed my hand.

"It's going to be fine."

I stared at the long silver tube as it filled with strangers. Fine is not how I would characterize this moment.

"Do you love her?" She stared up at me with those big raccoon eyes.

"I'll always love you if that's what you're asking."

Yet another eye roll. I was really racking them up.

"That's not what I'm asking," she said. "I know you love me, but do you love her?"

I rubbed my thumb over hers. "I guess so. I mean, yeah, I think so."

"You need to be sure." The way she set her mouth when she said that reminded me of her mother. Maria did that whenever she delivered a hard truth. Erin leaned in and narrowed her eyes. They almost disappeared into the dark pools of make-up. "Erika loves you, Dad. She told me a couple days ago."

"She did?"

Erin nodded. "She's super cool. I hope you feel the same about her."

"Why'd she tell you and not me?"

"Probably because you haven't said it, and she doesn't want to risk getting hurt."

I cocked my head. "When did you get so smart?"

"I'm not that smart. I'm just a good listener."

The television screen above us flicked to a breaking news story. A female reporter stood in front of an expensive-looking house with yellow crime scene tape strung behind her. The woman spoke into a microphone as a chyron scrolled along the bottom of the screen.

PROFESSIONAL BASEBALL PLAYER, CARLTON WINFREY, MURDERED IN COEUR D'ALENE, IDAHO.

"Shit," I muttered.

"Crap," Erin corrected. "It's better than saying shit."

A SUSPECT HAS BEEN DETAINED. FURTHER DETAILS AT 5:00 now ran across the screen's edge. When the news reporter ended her silent update, the program returned to another anchor in a studio somewhere.

I glanced down at Erin. She was concentrating on the bus.

Carlton Winfrey was tied to my former partner, Mike Davoli. His wife, Tina, had left him for the ballplayer. Mike and Tina had a daughter that was Erin's age. We all hung out together until Tina split with Carlton and took Jaime.

To stay near his daughter, Mike moved to Salt Lake City, where Winfrey played triple-A ball. Mike got on with the local police department before Los Angeles called up the ballplayer. When the three of them moved to California, Mike stayed in Utah. At least, that was the story I'd heard the last time I was in Seattle.

"It's my turn," Erin said excitedly and broke into my private thoughts. She slipped into my arms and hugged me. "What's wrong?"

"Nothing," I said.

"Are you sad I'm going?"

"Yeah."

"Then tell me."

I touched her cheek. "I'm sad you're going."

She beamed. "See? Feelings aren't so hard."

I kissed her on the forehead before she boarded the bus. Sending Erin home on a Tuesday morning seemed weird, but Maria had taken the opportunity to spend a week in Portland with her ailing mother. She'd only gotten home the previous evening.

Maybe it wasn't too late for me to get a bus ticket and ride with her. When the doors shut, I stopped my wishful thinking and went outside.

From my pocket, I pulled out a soft pack of cigarettes. I shook one free and lit it.

When Erin's bus pulled into view, I cupped the

cigarette and held it out of her sight. Along with swearing, my daughter wanted me to quit smoking.

From a middle seat, she smiled and waved. I waved back.

The bus pulled onto Sprague Avenue, then headed north on Browne Street toward the freeway.

***

On the main door to the house was a small, brass sign. *John Cutler Investigations*. With a twist of the knob, I was inside. The woman seated at the wooden desk lifted her gaze from the textbook she was reading.

Erika Taylor asked, "She get off okay?"

"Yeah."

June had been unseasonably warm, and we were fast closing in on July, which the meteorologists predicted would be hotter. The house was stuffy, even with the tall fan in the corner oscillating the air.

Erika pushed her textbook away and stood. She wore denim shorts and a t-shirt that left little to my imagination. Not that my imagination needed much encouragement because we'd been an item for a year now. She stepped around the desk, which took up a sizeable chunk of the small room. Her arms slipped around my neck and pulled me down toward her. Concern filled her eyes.

"You look sad."

"I'm fine."

"Are you, though?"

I shrugged. "Of course."

"Well, in that case." She released me and stepped back.

"In that case, what?"

"I was going to try and cheer you up, but if you're

already fine, I'll go back to what I was doing."

"No, wait." I mustered the best lascivious smile I could and waggled my fingers. "I can always use some cheering up."

"It's okay." She absently waved a hand, dropped into her chair, then pulled the textbook to her. "I've got studying to do."

I grunted and, even though her head was down, a smile appeared on her lips.

"Tease," I said.

"That's harassment," she muttered.

"Don't you have to be a paid employee for it to be harassment?"

"About that." Her eyes remained on the textbook.

A pile of bills sat on the corner of the desk. I thumbed through them. "Any calls?"

"Nuh-uh."

I dropped the envelopes without opening them. Looking at how much money I owed depressed me. Investigations seemed to be a sporadic business. I'd only been doing it for nine months so far, but it had all been small cases. None were glamorous or exciting.

The legitimate work mainly consisted of cheating spouses, photographs for divorce cases, or follow-up work for attorneys.

I did a couple of illegitimate jobs for a friend, but that dealt with finding stolen property that couldn't be reported to the cops.

The illicit work paid better but working with the lawyers made me feel most like a detective. There was a fine line between making the rent and keeping my morality intact. Erika helped around the office, which was nice but not necessary.

She was working on earning her degree while still working at Club Royale. She was taking summer courses to finish the four-year program in three years. She was almost done with her sophomore year and had intentions of earning a business degree. Erika hadn't settled on a specialty, but after putting school off for nearly a decade, she was determined to get it done now. The fact that her much younger brother had almost earned his degree bothered her. It certainly bothered her parents.

I kissed Erika on the cheek, then walked toward the back of the house. It was a small two-bedroom affair in the West Central neighborhood. The community center was next door.

Technically, I'm not sure if I could run a business from the house, but no one in the neighborhood had complained so far. While the rest of the county was on the upswing, this area—derogatorily known as Felony Flats—lagged. I rented the house for below market because the owner couldn't find a tenant with a clean record.

The house was larger than my former apartment but barely. There was an unfinished half-basement that I couldn't stand upright in. It was a place to toss any stuff I didn't care to keep but didn't want to throw away.

Erika spent a few nights here each week, but she still officially lived with her parents. And why wouldn't she? They had constructed an enormous apartment over their three-car garage. It resembled what I imagined a presidential suite might look like in a four-star hotel. The place put my home to shame.

I stepped into the backyard and sat on the steps. A faded cedar fence ran around the edge of the property and connected with a raggedy garage that appeared as if it were ready to collapse at any moment. The landlord didn't want to repair it, and I refused to put anything inside it. Anyone could break into the damn thing. The German shepherd rising from its position under one of the crab apple trees stopped someone from doing so.

Corporal stretched slowly, then ambled out of the shadows. He crossed the yard to push his head against my leg. I petted him. "Hey, pal."

We remained like that for a minute until he began panting. His hot breath warmed my leg. "Stop," I said unenthusiastically and pushed his head away. "You're making me hot."

A car drove along the dirt alley behind the house, kicking up dust and filling the quiet summer day with the rattle of a loose muffler.

Corporal's ears rose, and he craned his neck to follow the vehicle. When the car dropped out of the alley and faded into the distance, the dog found a shady spot to lay in.

Erika came outside and bent down. "I locked the front door," she whispered into my ear.

"What for?"

"Stop," she said unenthusiastically and pushed the back of my head. "You're making me hot."

She went back inside.

I looked at the dog. "Gotta go." I hurried after her.

***

After a final kiss, Erika said, "Don't be late."

"Do I have to?"

"This is important."

I lay on my back and stared at the ceiling. "Fine."

"Way to take one for the team."

Before I could think up a catty response, she slipped from the room. After the front door opened and closed, I sat upright and swung my feet off the side of the bed. My elbows rested on my knees as I contemplated our plans for the evening.

Simply put, I dreaded them. I needed to change my attitude.

I stood with a grunt, then dressed in a pair of shorts and shoes. When I stepped outside, Corporal loped over, and his tail wagged in wide arcs.

"Ready for some ball?"

He growled and jumped backward. The game was on. I led him through the gate and across the street to A.M. Cannon Park. The park came alive daily in the summer with kids and families. The swimming pool at its east end was a big part of the draw.

I threw a gnarled tennis ball as hard as I could, and the shepherd sprinted after it. He probably could have crushed it if he wanted, but he enjoyed the game as much as I did. He trotted back and dropped the slobbery orb at my feet.

"Good boy."

We played fetch for fifteen minutes, and then I ran him through his commands. His former owner had trained him in drill and ceremony—attention, parade rest, and the like. I took the dog in after the man's murder. Since I no longer lived downtown, I didn't have to walk Corporal every day, but I didn't want the dog to get rusty on those commands. They had saved my life once. Who knew if they might come in handy again?

After another fifteen minutes, the dog was waning fast. His tongue was out, and his tail was down. The summer heat was rough on him. We packed it in and headed home.

Inside, he immediately went to his water dish. While he

lapped that one dry, I refilled the monster-sized bowl he had outside. Upon securing the fence, I let the dog into the back where several trees kept most of the yard covered in shade.

"If anyone comes back here," I said, "eat them."

He lay in the coolest corner of the yard and panted. He wasn't interested in my jokes.

***

After a shower, I got dressed. While doing so, I turned on the television atop the bedroom dresser.

A news program had started, and a young reporter with squinty eyes and perfectly combed hair filled the screen. He tried to appear somber, but he had an irritating quality of smiling while he spoke. He was either excited to be at the crime scene, or he was new. He'd have to lose the grin soon, or he'd forever be assigned to covering state fairs and elementary school events.

"Tad Harrison reporting from Coeur d'Alene, Idaho. Earlier today, major league baseball player Carlton Winfrey was found murdered. Police have not released details of his death."

The television screen changed to a picture of a large home with a view of the lake behind it. Harrison continued to speak over the new image. *"Winfrey's body was found this morning at his home overlooking Lake Coeur d'Alene. He was vacationing here with his wife, Tina Winfrey, while rehabilitating a knee injury he suffered earlier in the season."*

A photo of Tina and Carlton Winfrey flashed on the screen. It seemed to be some sort of publicity shot and appeared to have been taken on a baseball field somewhere.

"*According to the police, Tina Winfrey discovered the twenty-six-year-old ballplayer in their home after returning from an early morning outing. One suspect was initially detained at a nearby Holiday Inn without incident. According to police, a Michael Dean Davoli was interviewed and then released.*"

I moved until I stood directly in front of the television. On the screen was a photograph of Davoli. Underneath the picture were the words 'Courtesy of the Salt Lake Police Department.'

The reporter continued his story. "*Mr. Davoli is the ex-husband of Tina Winfrey and had allegedly assaulted Winfrey the previous day after a run-in at a local bar. No police report of that incident was filed.*"

Now, a large, bespectacled man in a dark-blue uniform filled the screen. Under his face, the words 'Chief of Police Sanborn' were displayed. He spoke in the precise, practiced rhythm of police administrators.

"*Mr. Davoli was detained and questioned in connection with the homicide investigation. He denied any knowledge or involvement in this incident. There was an altercation between the two men, but Mr. Davoli does not appear to have been involved with the murder of Mr. Winfrey. He has been released but will remain a suspect until he is fully cleared by the evidence available to us.*"

Tad Harrison signed off his report with a final smile, and the news coverage flipped to a semi-truck accident on the freeway. I muted the television.

There was a time while working for the Seattle Police Department that Mike Davoli and I were close. He was the kind of guy I could confide in. I helped him through his divorce. He tried to help me through a period of darkness right before I lost my job, but I refused his outstretched hand. I wished I would have listened to him then.

Many things may have changed in my life over the past three years, but one thing hadn't—I still considered Davoli a friend.

I headed to the living room which doubled as my office. After grabbing a pencil and a paper pad from the desk, I picked up the telephone and dialed information.

Chapter 3

Erika's parents lived on the South Hill near Rockwood Boulevard and 22nd Avenue. The home was a white brick affair with large windows and a manicured front lawn.

I left my truck in the winding driveway. A wrought-iron screen door protected the house. In its middle was a circle containing the word *Taylor*. Every time I saw it, the same thought entered my mind—how much did something like that cost?

The front door opened without my ringing the bell. Carissa Taylor greeted me with a practiced smile. "Right on time." It didn't sound like a compliment.

She was an attractive woman with the same caramel-colored skin as Erika. As usual, Carissa appeared to have just stepped out of Nordstrom's catalog. A white blouse, light blue capri pants, and white sandals made an ensemble perfect for a high-society picnic. Her hair was moderately short, and her make-up was gracefully applied. Her gaze ran my length—much the way a cop assesses a suspect.

I smiled but remained silent. That was my survival tactic with Carissa.

She waved me in. As I passed by, she put her hand on my upper back. It didn't feel friendly or loving but instead guiding. "I believe Erika is in her apartment. Lonnie's in the back."

Even though Erika lived in a separate dwelling above the garage, the only entrances were through the house or by a staircase via the backyard. The rear door required going through the locked gate.

With a slight push on from Carissa, we headed down the hallway.

Each visit to the Taylor home impressed me. I'd been in nice houses before. My mother and her husband lived in one. I'd visited many elaborate homes while a police officer—rich people commit crimes just as much as they were victims.

But the Taylor household appeared always to be ready for a photoshoot. As if some fashion magazine might make a surprise visit, and Carissa Taylor refused to be caught off-guard. Lonnie Taylor once told me that even though he loved his wife, she was a woman of 'painfully expensive demands.' He also confided that Carissa had consulted a cadre of designers, yet she alone took credit for the home's appearance.

Carissa's hand dropped from my back. "Erika said that your daughter was lovely."

"Thank you."

I'm not sure what else I could say. Carissa had told Erika early on in our relationship that she didn't want her to see me. According to her mother, I had several strikes against me. From least offensive, I was six years older than her, a former cop, a private investigator with limited prospects, and white with a teenage daughter born out of wedlock.

Erika had shared those things with me after our first and particularly frosty visit to her parents' home. Things had warmed considerably with her father since that time, but not so much with her mother.

"It's nice they got along," Carissa said.

"Erin thought Erika was cool."

She raised an eyebrow. "Cool?"

I smiled politely.

We passed through the kitchen, where a fruit tray and side dishes already sat out. Through the sliding glass windows, Lonnie Taylor could be seen on the deck in front of a large silver barbeque. He seemed to be dancing. A faint stream of musical tones could be heard.

"And you're happy about that?"

I faced Carissa.

"That your daughter liked her for being cool?"

Hell, yeah, I was happy about it. My daughter was thirteen. Getting her to like anything seemed a significant accomplishment. The fact she liked my thirty-year-old girlfriend counted as a win in my book. What more could I hope for?

Carissa continued. "Erika says you're quite talkative, yet you're always so reserved around me. Do I put you off?"

"My mother once said that it was better to be silent and thought a fool."

Clarissa's eyes brightened. "Than to open your mouth and remove all doubt. Abraham Lincoln."

"She told me it was Mark Twain."

Her eyes darkened. "Of course, she did. I'll go see what's keeping Erika."

She left me at the sliding glass door.

I stepped out to the strains of Curtis Mayfield's "Freddie's Dead." Lonnie swayed with a pair of barbeque tongs in his hand. He wore a red apron over his blue polo shirt and khaki shorts. On the grill were five large steaks.

He spun around and grinned. "John Cutler."

We shook hands.

Lonnie extended the barbeque tongs toward a pitcher of iced tea. "Can I get you a glass?"

"No, thank you."

In the shade of an elm tree, at the back of the property was a white gazebo. Erika sat there with her brother, Isaiah. She noticed me and waved. We were too far apart to yell hello or any other type of greeting. I returned the wave.

Lonnie lowered the volume on the radio. "How's the investigating?"

"Not like the books."

"Nothing ever is." He turned back to the grill. "Hey, did you read any of the ones I recommended?"

After a previous dinner, Lonnie and I discussed our favorite books. He let it be known that he had an affinity toward mystery novels. I believe that's the primary reason he took an interest in my profession while Carissa disdained it.

"I did," I said. "*The Big Gold Dream.*"

He nodded approvingly. "Grave Digger Jones and Coffin Ed Johnson. Is that the one about the con man preacher?"

"It was."

"A short one if I remember correctly. A bit convoluted." He flipped a steak. "You should have started with *A Rage in Harlem.*"

"It was the only one I could find."

"No shit?" He flinched and glanced around, presumably for his wife. "Where did you find it?"

"That underground bookstore in downtown. The one that focuses on mysteries."

"I know the one. Lovely place. I've spent many an hour there."

"If you've got *Rage*, I'll read it."

He smiled. "Oh, I've got it, but I'm not loaning it out. No offense. Besides, that's part of the fun—hunting for a book. Don't you think?"

I shrugged.

"You disagree?" He waved the tongs. "To each their own. If I find another copy, I'll grab it for you. Mine was a gift." He flipped another steak. "So, what do you think about the state of our current police department?"

Books and music might have been what thawed the ice between Lonnie and me, but knowing that I could provide insight into how a police department functioned was what he genuinely liked. He enjoyed asking questions about a particular event or the occasional vague one just to start a conversation. This question was open-ended, so he likely had a deeper one waiting.

"I try not to think about it."

Lonnie turned another steak, then pushed on it with the tongs. "There was an article in the *Journal of Business*. Did you see it?"

"I don't get the *Journal*."

"They interviewed the guild president and the chief. Both trotted out that exhausted argument of cops being overwhelmed with calls for service. How they need more men, more equipment, and more training, which always equates to more money."

"It's about the only thing the union and the administration align on."

"Isn't that the truth?" He poked another of the steaks. "To stoke the neighborhoods into supporting the push for new hires, they bang the drum of fear."

"What other drum are they going to bang? The drum of success? If they told the people they were crushing crime, there wouldn't be a need for more. At best, the argument would be for maintaining the status quo."

"And the status quo won't get Officer Friendly a troop

transport."

Lonnie had made his position clear in previous conversations that the local police force was too militarized. I saw a similar trend in Seattle, and it seemed to be one sweeping the nation—cops looking like soldiers.

"When the police act like an occupying army," Lonnie continued, "the citizens will be the enemy."

"And don't try to take away those toys now."

He cast a sideways glance. "Nine-eleven?"

"Terrorism has finally come to our shores."

Lonnie angrily clacked his tongs. "Terrorism has been on these shores since the founding. And you don't have to look too far back for examples. Oklahoma City. The Olympic Park Bombing. Hell, don't forget all those school and workplace shootings. Always angry white boys with misplaced hostilities."

"You're proving their point."

Lonnie's hand dropped to his side. "How's that?"

"They need those fancy weapons to protect us."

"So, every time something bad happens, we call for more cops? That seems the easy thing to do."

"The whole thing has gotten worse after the towers fell. Even questioning it brings accusations of a lack of patriotism. Especially with everyone blathering on about 'thank you for your service.'"

Lonnie's jaw flexed. "Now, hold on. I've said that plenty of times myself."

"A lot of people do, but have you given it any thought when you did? No, right? You just saw a uniform and blurted out thank you. A whole nation of parrots. But what was everyone really saying? Thank you for protecting me because I can't protect myself."

His face flattened. "I wasn't saying that, John."

"Yet, that's what they heard because, in the mind of a cop, citizens are sheep who need protecting."

The conversation's joy had left Lonnie, and his face had hardened. "I'm not a sheep. They are mindless, bleating beasts."

"Helpless and ripe for the kill by waiting, hungry wolves. That's why we, the flock, need the sheepdog. That's the shit that cops tell themselves. They preach it to their rookies. They get it at seminars. They hear it on in-service days—day in, day out. Like a mantra—citizens are sheep, and criminals are wolves. If you repeatedly dehumanize and vilify entire swaths of the population, what do you think the eventual ramifications are?"

Lonnie smacked the tongs against the edge of the grill. "Goddamn." He didn't bother looking around for Carissa. He repeated his expletive.

"The whole law enforcement fairy tale pisses me off."

He eyed me with some suspicion. "But you were part of it."

"Getting run over by their machine tends to change your attitude."

Lonnie cocked his head. "Oh, does it now? I would never have guessed." Laughing with a mocking tone, he turned toward the grill and moved the meat to the higher rack. "Are you glad you left?"

I waited for him to finish before answering. When he faced me, I said, "It's a drug."

"What is?"

"The thin blue line. Once it's in your system, it's hard to get out—even when it's bad for you."

Lonnie's brow furrowed as if he were concentrating on my words.

"When things get lonely," I continued, "that us-versus-them mentality is attractive—especially out here where no one stands together.”

“Some of us do.”

I understood what he meant. Some stood together, often in the face of persecution. It was usually based upon a shared struggle, whether it be race, religion, or sexual preference, but the fight always needed a higher power to band people together.

But for a straight white male, what was a calling to rally around?

The church required a belief in God and the suspension of reason.

The white power movement required a belief in the race’s superiority and the suspension of common sense.

The biker gangs required a commitment to an outlaw lifestyle and the suspension of regular bathing.

The cops simply required a conviction that they alone were order in a world of chaos and the suspension of any belief that they were infallible. It was delusional and wrong, but it was an attitude needed for war in the streets.

And this I wouldn’t admit to Lonnie—I missed the war.

I was mad at the decisions that led to me being kicked out of the blue fraternity. Most of my anger was directed at myself, but occasionally I pointed it at the organization I believed betrayed me.

The sliding glass door opened, and Carissa came out. “Lon, have you seen Erika? I checked her apartment.”

He pointed the tongs toward the back of the property. “She’s with Isaiah.”

Carissa nodded. “Do you gentlemen need anything?”

“We’re good,” Lonnie said.

The sliding glass door closed as Carissa disappeared back inside.

"I appreciate your thoughts," Lonnie said. "You've given me some things to think about."

According to Erika, her father grew up poor, yet worked his way through college then medical school before becoming a doctor. Even though they lived in this lovely home, Lonnie never flaunted his wealth or social position. He was always kind, and I genuinely liked him. His wife might not have approved of me, but I honestly hoped Lonnie did.

"Will you get Erika and Isaiah?" he asked. "The steaks are almost ready."

I headed straight for the gazebo through the large, well-maintained lawn. Lonnie had once told me he purchased the home almost twenty years ago. With the hot housing market Spokane experienced, I couldn't imagine what it might be worth now.

Just as I made it to the little hut, Erika's younger brother stepped out. He was a big man who played football for the local university. He expected to be the starting tailback this year. His brown eyes went flat, and we passed each other.

"Isaiah," I said.

He muttered something I pretended not to catch.

While Carissa hid her displeasure at my dating Erika, Isaiah did no such thing. It wasn't that I was white that earned his ire. Isaiah dated only white girls and hung out with mostly white friends. It was that Isaiah had gotten in trouble with Club Royale while I was working the floor. As a result, he'd been banned. Getting barred from the hottest nightclub while still young was something he couldn't forgive me for.

But it was his friend who had hit me with a beer bottle—an act that Isaiah tried to cover up. The scar hidden under my hair wouldn't allow me ever to forget. Both

Isaiah and his friend avoided getting arrested for the assault, but what mattered most was getting 86'd from the club. Misplaced hostilities, as Lonnie might say.

"I'm sorry about him," Erika said.

"Don't worry about it."

She sat cross-legged on one of the cushioned benches. A single elm tree provided shade for the little wooden structure. Erika held a book in her lap and smiled. I leaned in and kissed her.

"How was mother?" she asked.

"The usual."

"And I suppose dad asked you something to spark a conversation. What was it?"

I sat next to her and rested my back against a wooden rail. "Books." I grabbed the edge of hers to get a peek at the cover. "Speaking of, what are you reading?"

"*Fundamentals of Economics*." She closed the textbook.

"Light reading." The smell of grilling meat floated on the late June breeze. "Steaks are ready."

"I figured. Did you do anything after I left?"

I slipped my hand into hers. "Laid in bed and drifted away on thoughts of you."

She frowned *and* furrowed her brow—the double-barreled signal for her disbelief.

"Okay," I said. "Corporal and I went to the park and played some ball."

Her face relaxed. "That dog. I took him over, too. You think he'd be tired." She leaned closer. "Something's bothering you. Was it something my dad said?"

"No."

"My mom?"

"C'mon. Let's go."

I started to stand, but she pulled me back to the bench. "Tell me."

"Have you seen the news?"

"Not really."

"There was a murder in Coeur d'Alene."

"Oh. I think I did hear something about that. Someone famous."

I stood. "A baseball player."

"So, he is famous."

"Kind of."

She cocked her head. "How can a baseball player only be kind of famous?"

"Let's go," I said. "Your dad's waving at us, and I'm hungry."

She stood. "Who was murdered?"

"Carlton Winfrey."

As we left the gazebo, she said, "I've never heard of him."

"You wouldn't. Only fans of the game will know him."

"How's that?"

"Because he's a utility player. He's got great defensive skills but can't hit very well. The team keeps him on the roster for certain situations."

She stopped and yanked my hand, sending me in an arc to face her. "You're not a fan of baseball. How do you know him?"

"Mike Davoli."

"Who?"

"We used to be partners in Seattle."

"Oh, right. You've mentioned him."

"The Coeur d'Alene Police questioned him about Winfrey."

We started walking again.

"This Ravioli guy is up here?" Erika asked.

"Davoli," I corrected.

"How did he get here? And how does he know Winfrey? I'm confused. I think you skipped something."

"Several years ago, Mike's wife left him for Carlton."

Erika stopped walking again. "Oh. So, wait. Ravioli—"

"Davoli."

"Never got over his wife's leaving him and followed them to Coeur d'Alene?"

"That's making short work of it, but yeah."

"Stalk much?"

"Huh?"

She started walking and pulled me along. "Sounds like your friend did it."

"How so?"

"He traveled across a full state, and the wife's new husband ends up dead. Easy case for the police, in my opinion."

"The cops interviewed Mike and let him go."

Erika eyed me. "They did?"

"That's what the news said."

"The cops think he's innocent even after stalking his wife over a full state?"

"I'm not sure he stalked her."

We were almost to the back deck, and she stopped again. "Are you going to reach out to him?"

"I tried. According to the news, he was picked up at a Holiday Inn. There are only a couple in the area, so I left messages for him."

From the deck, Lonnie said, "Hurry up, you two. Isaiah is almost done with his steak, and now he's eyeing yours."

***

After dinner, Erika headed to a study group, and I returned home. There was one message on the answering machine.

"Hey, John, it's Maria. I picked up Erin in Ellensburg. We're home safely now. No need to call."

She might have said there wasn't a need, but I grabbed the phone. Maria answered on the second ring.

"Hello?" It sounded as if she was moving around. Silverware clattered in the background.

"It's John."

"Oh, hey. You didn't need to call."

"I know. How did she like it?"

More clattering now. "She loved it. Sorry about the noise. We just got done with dinner, and I'm doing the dishes. I guess I should stop. I'll stop. Oh my God, wait until you hear her stories."

"About the people she rode with?"

"Yes, but she even had some about the stops they made along the way. The one in Moses Lake was hysterical." She pronounced it *hah*-sterical. Maria clearly enjoyed our daughter's tales of riding the bus. "I'll let her tell you."

"What's she doing now?"

"Taking a shower. She just got in. She'll be in there for half an hour. I'll have her call later."

"Okay," I said. "And thanks for letting her come and stay."

"I'm glad you got some time together. It's good for her."

"Good for me, too."

There was a pause before Maria said, "She liked your girlfriend."

"Yeah, they got along okay."

"She said she's young."

"Not that young."

"Younger than you."

"By a couple years, but we all can't share the same birthday."

"I'm not judging," Maria said. "That's just what she called out."

I stayed quiet. If that was the only thing my daughter pointed out, I was proud of her.

Sort of wistfully, Maria said, "I don't think she's ever called me cool."

"No? She thinks I'm cool."

Maria chuckled, "Of course, she does. Good night, John."

"Good night."

After all these years, Maria and I had maintained a friendly relationship which is saying something. We dated a few times before she became pregnant. When I offered to marry her, she refused. She told me flatly that I wasn't the marrying type, and she didn't want to get into a relationship she knew would later backfire. That hurt, but it was the best for us all, including Erin.

Maria must have sensed I wasn't ready to be a father. It took a lot of years for me to understand that. Oh, I sent child support payments, but I had been remiss beyond that. I tried to make up for it, but I have got a long way to go.

I grabbed the James Crumley novel I recently purchased at a used bookstore and headed outside. Corporal hurried over and sat next to me as I reclined on the back steps.

The Last Good Kiss was about a detective hired to find a derelict author. After locating him, the two men set out to trace a woman who's been missing for more than a decade. The detective was based in Montana, which was only two borders away. I'd been through the state a few times, so the setting in the novel felt oddly recognizable. There was an extra jolt of familiarity when the detective mentioned watching a broadcast television station from Spokane. I don't know why that pleased me as I'd only been in the city for a couple of years. I even called out the passage to the dog. He seemed unimpressed.

The unmistakable *thump-thump-thump* of a Harley-Davidson engine entered the neighborhood. Those sounds weren't uncommon. Loud bikes, unmufflered cars, or train whistles were all sounds of a West Central night.

When the engine came to a pause, though, I closed my book, and Corporal's ears raised. It sounded as if the motorcycle might be in front of the house. The bike soon turned off, and the stillness of the evening returned.

The dog stood and moved toward the fence. He appeared to stiffen as he looked through the slats.

From inside the house, the doorbell rang.

Now, it was my turn to stand. I opened the back door and said, "Fall in." Unknown motorcycle riders would be greeted with additional security measures. Corporal trotted to my side, and we entered the house.

I stopped at the desk and traded Crumley's book for a gun. Then I checked the peephole.

Facing the dog, I said, "Parade rest." He dropped to his haunches and kept his eyes alertly on me.

On the front step stood Michael Davoli. He wore blue jeans and a black leather jacket. His short hair was messy, no doubt from the shiny, black helmet he carried. Several days of stubble covered his face.

"Cutler," he said with a fading smile. His eyes dropped

to the Glock dangling by my side. "Nice to see you, too."

"Mike." I tucked the gun into the back of my jeans, and we shook hands.

He started into the house but stopped. "Jesus, John. Guns and a guard dog. I've heard Spokane was rough, but wow."

"He won't bite."

"You sure?"

I turned to the dog. "At ease."

Unimpressed by the visitor, Corporal wandered toward the back of the house.

Mike tapped the door under the *John Cutler Investigations* sign. "Got yourself a new profession."

I nodded.

"Going well?"

"Seems to be." He didn't need to know the struggles of a fledgling business.

After he entered, he started to shut the door.

"Leave it open," I said. "Let the night air in."

In the corner, the oscillating fan pushed the air around.

Mike sat in one of the chairs for clients. He put his helmet on the floor near his foot. "Is this what you've been up to since you left Seattle? You disappeared one afternoon. Your cell phone went dead. No one heard from you again."

"I needed to get my head right."

"And now?"

"I'm good."

Mike rested his foot on top of the helmet. "Did you see the news?"

"I did."

"Got any beer?"

I waved for him to follow, and we headed into the

kitchen. Corporal had been lying on the cool linoleum floor. I let the dog into the backyard then pulled two beers from the fridge.

"Thanks," Mike said and popped the top. He tilted the can back and took a long drink. When he was done, he wiped his mouth with the back of his hand. "What?"

"I'm trying to wrap my head around you standing in my kitchen. What are you doing up here?"

"You-know-who had a place in Coeur d'Alene. I guess it's a hot spot for second homes."

"From what I hear."

"Assholes with too much money." He toasted me with his beer. "Am I right?"

I folded my arms and leaned against the refrigerator. He hadn't answered my question yet about his purpose for being in the area.

Even in just a few moments, I could tell that our dynamic had changed. Either it was him or me, but we were different. Back in the department, we could share an easy laugh or help the other through a difficult situation. It had been a little more than three years since I'd seen the guy, but now he seemed more stranger than friend.

"Anyway," Mike continued, "The sonofabitch was up here rehabbing his knee. Tore his ACL sliding into second. Third game of the season." His lip curled. "Served him right."

"You followed his career?"

"Not because I'm a fan." He kicked back the beer for another drink. "Hard not to pay attention after she left me for him."

He shook his beer can. I hadn't even taken a sip from mine, and his sounded almost empty.

"Why are you up here?" I asked again.

"The sixty-four-thousand-dollar question."

"Seems so."

His smile was mirthless. "Tina and I have been talking."

"Talking?"

He nodded. "Over the past year."

"Like talking *talking*? As in, she's calling *you*?"

"Don't look at me like I'm making this shit up. We used to be married. The woman knows I get her."

"But—"

"But nothing. She needed someone to confide in, so she called me. It's as simple as that. Things had gotten bad with what's his nuts."

"And Tina didn't have a girlfriend to call?"

"What's with you?" Mike asked.

"Seems weird. Calling her ex-husband and all."

"We're friends now. She can't want to talk with me?"

I didn't believe it. Tina might be able to be friends with Mike, but he could never be friends with her. He hadn't been able to let go of her after she left him for Winfrey.

"So," Mike said, "they had been arguing more and more."

"But she called *you* to talk about it."

He cast a sideways glance. "What are you saying?"

"You didn't call her?"

His face pinched. "And get her in trouble? No fucking way."

It sounded as if he was having an emotional affair with his ex-wife. Maybe it was a two-way street, and Tina was getting the same thing out of it. Perhaps she was in a quasi-domestic violence situation with her new husband, so she reached out to rekindle something with her former husband—even if it would only be recycled emotions.

"What about Jaime?" I asked. "Do you call her?"

"Whenever I want. She's got her own phone. That prick couldn't stop me from talking to my daughter. He may not like it, but I don't care."

"Where's Jaime now?"

"With Tina's mother in Port Orchard. Riding horses for the month and having the time of her life. Thank God she wasn't around when that nigger got murdered."

The word slapped me, and the resulting sting lingered. My face warmed, and I stared at Mike.

His eyes narrowed. "Now what?"

"You've never said that before."

"Said what?"

"The N-word."

"Are you for real?"

"I'm serious."

Mike smirked. "You never spoke up before when anyone said it."

If he was talking about guys in the department, then he was right. I hadn't. But no one had ever used a racist term so blatantly. And I sure as hell didn't want it used in my house—especially now.

"Hell," he said, "Maybe you said the same thing about that crack dealer who jammed you up."

"I never said it."

"I think you did."

My hands balled. "No. I didn't. Not once."

He tossed his empty beer can into the sink. It clanged when it hit. "You said something close. I don't remember what it was, but I'm sure you did."

I shook my head.

"Are you a choir boy now? Left the badge behind and became better than the rest of us? Maybe you're a goddamned democrat, too. Is that it? Have you turned your back on the job?"

"Do me a favor," I said through gritted teeth. "Shut the fuck up."

"I see you didn't leave your anger behind."

I inhaled deeply, then whispered, "Please."

"Oh, am I supposed to stop talking now?"

I raised a hand to cut off the conversation. "Let's forget it."

"Forget nothing. I'm not ever forgetting what happened." He pointed east. "That Mandigo motherfucker ruined my life. He took my wife. Took my daughter. I had to follow them to be a part of their lives. It was a constant game of one-upmanship with that—"

I pushed him, and he stumbled back.

"The fuck?" he said.

"Knock it off."

"You knock it off. As far as I'm concerned, the black bastard got what he deserved."

The way he said it made my skin crawl. "What happened to you?"

"Nothing happened to me. You were a cop. You know this as well as anyone. There are blacks, and then there are—"

I shoved him to the floor.

He got to his feet, and his face reddened. "You *are* a goddamned democrat. I knew it. Are you contributing to the NAACP, too? Walking around reciting that I-have-a-dream bullshit?"

"Leave."

"What?"

"Go."

His face softened. "But you said to get in touch. The message you left at the hotel."

"That was for a friend."

Confusion flashed in his eyes.

I pointed at the door. "Now."

"But—"

"Get out!"

He walked over to the desk and picked up his helmet. As soon as he cleared the threshold, I slammed the door and locked it.

Several moments passed before his motorcycle fired up.

Chapter 4

The following morning, Wednesday, Erika stopped by. She wore denim shorts and a tight, red t-shirt.

I was behind the office desk with the newspaper spread out. The oscillating fan was already hard at work in the corner.

"Ugh," she grunted. "The paper."

"Every morning."

"Why?"

"There's a big world out there with stuff happening in it."

She dropped into the chair in front of the desk. "Pay attention to me."

"Inna minute."

"Now."

I leaned further over the paper and did my best to ignore Erika. However, I could still see her as she turned and draped her legs over the chair's arm. Her skin glimmered as if lotion had been recently applied.

"Pay attention to me," she repeated.

"Nuh-huh."

I furrowed my brow and focused on a small article about Carlton Winfrey. His death was on the front page of the regional section. The details about his murder were still vague, but it seemed a witness had stepped forward with unsolicited information. This development had led to a new, unidentified suspect with both motive and opportunity.

Erika rubbed a leg and asked, "How was your night?"

"Fine."

"Mine was boring. Study group, remember?"

I moved on to an article about Newman Lake's milfoil problem. I didn't know what milfoil was, and the paragraph I had just read didn't make any sense. But I didn't dare look up and let Erika win the attention game. I squinted and tried to understand why milfoil was an issue.

"You know how they are," she said. "A bunch of smart people together. Blah blah blah. So stupid. That's funny. Smart people being stupid. Anyway, more wasted time than helpful. Did you do study groups when you were in college?"

I grunted an affirmative response. Now, the last sentence I read didn't make any sense at all—something about dichlorophenoxyacetic acid and dimethylamine salt.

"I can't imagine you being in a study group," Erika said. "Maybe it's just me." She stretched her legs into the air and pointed her toes. Even though she was a petite woman, sitting sideways in the small chair seemed incredibly uncomfortable. Her hand dragged lazily along a leg as if she were showing off a new car at some auto convention. "If we were in a study group together, I'd be all twitterpated being around you."

"Uh-huh," I muttered. The words in the newspaper were simply ink splotches now.

"Twitterpated. That's from *Bambi*. I bet you didn't know that."

I struggled to contain the smile creeping out from the edges of my lips.

"So, instead of studying, I'd probably be distracted thinking about jumping your bones."

I looked up.

"I win." She laughed and spun in her chair. She

drummed her hands on the edge of the desk. "What are we doing today? Got anything to work on?"

Folding the newspaper, I said, "Nope."

"Oh." She flopped back into her chair. "What about your friend? Did he call?"

"He stopped by."

"And?"

"And nothing."

She leaned forward. "How's he doing?"

"Fine."

Erika cocked her head. "I asked how last night was, and you said fine, but you didn't tell me your friend stopped by until now. Then I ask how he's doing, and you say fine. Why do I get the feeling it was less than fine?"

I shrugged.

"It's been years since you've seen him, right? Did he look like you remembered?"

"Pretty much."

"What did you talk about?"

"Not much."

"He was interviewed as a suspect in a murder, and you don't talk about anything? I thought you guys were best friends."

"Partners," I said. "That's it."

"You've mentioned this guy before like you were friends. Something happened."

"Nothing happened."

"I want to know."

"There's nothing to know. We don't have much in common."

"But his ex-wife's husband was murdered. How did he feel about it?"

"Not bad." My gaze drifted to the folded paper.

"I guess that's to be expected." Erika stood. "You're not paying attention to me."

"I'm sorry."

"Want some help around here?"

"Not much to do."

"In that case, why don't you take the dog for a walk? When you get back, maybe we can…"

"Can what?"

"If I have to tell you, I must be doing it wrong."

I rolled out of my chair. "Let's do that first, and then I'll take the dog."

"No," she said. "You're head's not in the right spot. Wouldn't be any fun for me. Walk the dog. Then love me."

***

While the dog and I walked, I tried to be productive and think about work.

The pipeline was dry. All I had left to do was return the ring Terry took to its owner. Unfortunately, Marian Howell wasn't due back until Sunday. There was nothing else active. While Erin was visiting, a couple of calls had come in from an attorney I worked with, but I passed on them.

Most jobs took days, if not weeks, to resolve. That meant I'd need to prime the pump again if I wanted work to start flowing. I did that initially when I opened the shop. Asking for work with my hand out wasn't one of my favorite things. However, eating with a roof over my head was.

Corporal and I headed southeast. The neighborhoods grew rougher as we got closer to the police station. Even though patrol cars rolled in and out of the area at all hours of the day, the reported crime rate was astronomical in that section of town. It didn't take a genius to figure out why.

Four entities shared the same West Central campus—the Spokane Public Safety Building, the Spokane County Jail, Juvenile Court Services, and the county courthouse. The PSB is home to the city police and the county sheriff's department. Juvenile Detention is located within the neighboring JCS building.

As residents in the neighborhood accumulated wealth, they left behind those four structures. And who could fault them? Most folks inside those buildings are either criminals or associated with an industry devised to stop those crooks. It's an age-old problem of NIMBY—Not in My Back Yard.

The second reason for the high crime rate related directly to the jail. When a detainee is released, they are dumped right into the West Central neighborhood. The highest concentration of ne'er-do-wells was in this neighborhood courtesy of a taxi service known as law enforcement.

Corporal and I avoided cutting through the PSB campus. Instead, we walked its outskirts. Better to take a long way around. I'm not a suspicious man, but less police contact is good.

And in the back of my mind was the tirade I'd spouted at the Taylor house. Lonnie might have agreed with most of it, but I should have kept my mouth shut. I tended to do that—speak first, think second, and regret third. Maybe if I thought initially, I could avoid the aftertaste of remorse.

I laughed at the folly of my introspection, and the dog looked up. Nearby, a woman who had the clothing and demeanor of a lawyer eyed me. She frowned disapprovingly and stepped back. It wasn't for fear of the dog. Men who openly snicker at themselves should be considered suspect.

We continued into Riverfront Park, which is in the heart of downtown. The Spokane River flowed through its middle. The winter runoff would rage through the park during the spring, its anger and fury combining into a beautiful display for all to see. Today, the water was almost still—the sad result of an upriver dam.

Seeing the carousel brought back the fun I'd had with my daughter. I paused long enough to remember her happiness as she reached for a ring. Each loop around brought more laughter as she pursued the brass one.

Corporal and I stopped near the opera house on the far side of the park. After freeing the dog from his leash, he headed into a forested area. I lay on the grass and stared up into the blue sky.

My musings eventually drifted to Mike Davoli. When he left last night, my thoughts were overwhelmed with him. Before falling asleep, I came to an uneasy peace with the entire conflict. Seeing Erika made his comments real again.

The guy inside my house was not the man I remembered. He'd changed in an angry way. He never said anything overtly racist while we were friends. Maybe he told an off-color joke a time or two. Most people did, regardless of race, regardless of gender.

As cops, we all used words or phrases we knew were inappropriate in polite company. Some guys used them too much. Others used them only for specific types of people. There was a female officer who repeatedly referred to gay men as fags—or worse. She was a lesbian, and all the guys respected her. I did. She was one of the best cops I ever worked with. Because of that, none of us ever thought to correct her language. And why would we? Not only would doing so be suspect but it could also have been seen as weak. Correcting her also meant we would have to be on guard for every little thing we said and did.

Plenty of guys looked the other way because they knew they weren't perfect. It was simply the pot calling the kettle black. Or in this case, the N-word.

Tina's leaving Mike changed him. He used to be a fun guy to be around. Maybe he still was, I don't know. At this point, I didn't care. The guy who showed up wasn't a friend. How could he be? Not only would I never condone the things he said, but the woman I was with now represented the things he hated. The whole thing was ugly.

Corporal came over and sat with his nose only inches from my head. He panted into my ear. I turned and faced him directly. "Ready to go home?"

He sniffed me twice, then sneezed in my face.

***

A block away, I noticed it—a motorcycle parked in front of my home.

Corporal sensed my anxiety and dropped lower. His head swiveled to find the danger. Our walk turned into a trot, and the dog made excited noises.

At the house, we went around the side and quietly entered the backyard. When the gate closed, I unleashed the dog.

On the backstep, no sounds were coming from inside. I stepped into the kitchen, and Corporal remained at my side. Low voices seemed to be engaged in polite conversation.

"Parade rest," I said, and the dog sat.

In the living room, Mike was in one of the customer chairs. He held his helmet in his lap. Erika sat behind the desk.

Never taking my eyes off Mike, I asked, "What's going on?"

Mike opened his mouth, but Erika interrupted him.

"Your friend dropped by." Her voice sounded hollow, and the smile she wore was plastic.

I faced her now. She didn't look happy. She wasn't mad, either. Instead, her expression was simply blank—that of a master poker player. But that was enough of a tell for me.

"I can't help you, Mike."

"You two should talk." Erika stood. "Besides, I'm late for an appointment."

"What appointment?" I asked.

As she passed by the desk, Erika said to Mike, "It was nice to meet you." Her words were as flat as her appearance. She stuck out her hand, and he politely shook it. It was the handshake at the end of a blind date gone wrong.

Erika paused near the door. "I'll call you later." She spun and was out the door.

My gaze shifted to Mike. "What did you say?"

"Nothing."

"Couldn't have been nothing."

He shrugged. "I swear. I didn't say anything. We were only talking a few minutes before you got home."

I dropped into my chair and rubbed my face. "You shouldn't be here."

"But I need your help."

"You still haven't told me why you're in Coeur d'Alene."

Mike put his helmet on the floor. "Tina called."

"And?"

"Some bad guys started hanging around, and she was worried."

I leaned forward. "Bad guys? Really?"

"Okay. They were associates of Winfrey. He dismissed her concerns by saying they were childhood friends."

"She was married to a cop. She had to tell you more than that."

"They're bangers."

The way he said it felt racist, and it put me on the edge of the previous night's fight. "Did she call them that? *Bangers*."

He lifted an apologetic hand. "She said they looked like trouble, but she did not say they were bangers. But the guys hanging around Winfrey are confirmed gangsters. That's a fact."

I flopped back in my chair. "It's athletic chic to look like you run with a crew. Some players even claim an affiliation."

"Winfrey's the real deal." He rolled his eyes. "*Was* the real deal."

"How's that?"

"I asked our gang task force to reach out to their counterparts in LA."

"Salt Lake has gangs?"

"Just because Mormon central is lily-white doesn't mean there's not a bunch of idiots who can't play hard." He made his thumb and forefinger into a gun and held it sideways. "Bang bang. Remember how it was?"

I did, but I couldn't determine if what he was intimating was racist or simply a reflection of real life. In Spokane County, an area that was roughly ninety percent white, I'd seen many young black and Hispanic men who appeared to be in gangs. However, hundreds of white men dressed and acted the same way. Since I was no longer a cop, I had no way of telling who was actually in a gang and who wasn't.

Was I viewing everything Mike said through the lens of his racism? I didn't want to go down that rabbit hole, so I stayed away from it. "What did the task force find out?"

"Winfrey grew up in Los Angeles. In the early nineties, he ran with a local sect called the Dead Boys. Strange name for a crew." Mike shifted in his chair. "Anyway, when Winfrey was younger, he got popped for a few chippy crimes—theft, mischief, misdemeanor assault," he ticked them off on his fingers, "but he was smart enough to stay away from anything heavy-duty. Supposedly, his parents pushed him into sports, and the kid earned a baseball scholarship to USC. After he graduated, he got drafted late by the Mariners and ended up playing with the Tacoma Rainers."

"All that from the gang unit."

He moved his head as if trying to pop a crick in his neck. "I did some additional background. He's been sort of my project for the past couple years."

"Has he had any police contact since getting drafted?"

"A couple DWB stops while in Tacoma, but nothing ever came of them." The Driving While Black comment rolled off his tongue as if he were laying out a grocery list. "He never touched the radar in Salt Lake."

"You didn't stop him?"

Mike's brow furrowed. "And risk losing access to my kid? Uh, no way, thank you. I may have hated the sonofabitch, but I wasn't going to lose my career and my daughter over him."

"Didn't you ever go to one of Jaime's school events when both of you were there?"

"I ate plenty of shit because of that guy. Seeing him there with Tina." Mike closed his eyes. "But I knew there would come a day." He opened his eyes and smiled. "And it did."

I shook my head.

"You're saying I can't be happy he's dead?"

"Doesn't feel right."

"He didn't steal your wife."

"Tina's got some blame in this. You, too."

"Are you some sort of counselor now?"

I wasn't. I had told Terry the same thing. "Sorry."

Mike averted his gaze. "Yeah. Me, too."

Silence hung in the room before I prompted, "Back to Carlton."

"Where was I?"

"No law enforcement contact in Salt Lake."

"Right," he said. "Well, that changed when the Angels called him up. He pinged at the edge of LAPD's radar." He snapped his fingers. "Winfrey avoided most of the hardcore scene, and nothing more than a traffic infraction was issued."

"What did the gang unit think was going on?"

"Some hustlers from Winfrey's childhood started hanging around. You know, smoking and joking. That type of thing. But the gang unit thought the Dead Boys were grooming Winfrey for access to the majors. I didn't buy it, though."

"How come?"

"I hated the guy, no doubt—"

"No doubt," I agreed.

He smirked. "But Winfrey wasn't about to sling drugs

in the clubhouse. The guy wanted to play in the majors. I'd read and watched a lot of interviews with him. He seemed genuine about his appreciation for the game."

"Did Tina say anything else about these friends?"

"That they didn't trust her. They would go into different rooms to talk with Winfrey."

"Were these guys around in Tacoma or Salt Lake?"

Mike shook his head. "They didn't appear until California—when he moved home. At first, they only showed up now and then. After a while, it was almost daily. Again, this is what she said. The gang unit only had some of this."

"Did you pass along this intel?"

Mike glanced away again.

He hadn't. Had he, the information might have proven useful. If Carlton Winfrey ended up arrested from information leaked via Mike, Tina would never forgive him. Better to hold what he learned close to the vest so that he could continue to talk with her.

But what could Mike really give the gang unit? They already knew Winfrey was in contact with the Dead Boys. The cops suspected, although perhaps wrongly, that the crew wanted access to the majors. Mike holding any information back might have been self-serving, but it certainly wasn't damaging to LAPD's surveillance.

"So," I said, "you and Tina continued to talk."

"And she called once to complain about Winfrey. Said he was changing. She blamed the guys that were hanging around."

"How was Winfrey changing?"

He shrugged. "I didn't care. I offered to come to California and get her and Jaime, but she told me no. Then she downplayed the whole thing. Said she just wanted someone to talk with."

"And you were happy it was you that she turned to."

Mike waved a hand. "Of course, I was happy, and I don't care if it was wrong. She was talking to me. That's all that mattered. She called some more when they moved up here."

"Don't most guys stay with the team when they're rehabbing? Sort of a team unity thing?"

"How would I know? Maybe baseball is different, especially when the guy is out for the season."

I inhaled deeply and held it. Mike waited as I studied him. I hadn't wanted him back in my house, and I should have kicked him out immediately. But I didn't. Part of me wanted him to be the friend I remembered. I exhaled. "Now that I've got the backstory on Tina and Carlton, what about you? How'd you get up here?"

"Some of the Dead Boys followed Winfrey."

"Why?"

"He needed an entourage, I guess. Tina *really* didn't like that. LA is big, but this area is small. Hell, you know that. Because of it, the guys were always around. Weeks passed, and shit got worse. I kept telling Tina to go back to California, but she wouldn't listen. Instead, she tried to get Winfrey to break free of his friends. Dude got pissed and slapped her around. Bruised her up pretty good."

"Was that the first time?"

"As far as I know."

"And that's when you came?"

"You bet I did."

"What did you think you were going to do?"

"Set the sonofabitch straight."

I crossed my arms. "The news said you got your chance."

"She was still bruised when I arrived, and I lost my head. I confronted the bastard outside a nightclub, but a couple of his boys intervened. Some local cops were already nearby and broke it up before anything more than some pushing and shoving could happen. They told us all to get lost."

"If he hit her, why wouldn't Tina leave?"

"You saw it when you were a cop. A guy smacks his woman around then apologizes. Says everything is his fault and promises to change. He'll never do it again. Yada yada yada. All bullshit."

"But now he's dead and can't hurt her again, so you can go home. Why are you still hanging around?"

"That's the problem. I can't go." Mike leaned forward. "Tina's been arrested. She's being charged with Winfrey's murder."

Chapter 5

"Why do the cops suspect Tina?" I asked.

"Because she found his body." Mike threw his hands in the air. "That's their case."

"There's got to be more."

"With these locals? Proximity and relationship are all they've got."

I pulled a notepad closer. "That's not enough."

"I agree, but *they* made the arrest—not me."

"How was he murdered? The news didn't say."

"I don't know, but I got the feeling by the questions they were asking me that it was up close and personal."

"Like with a knife?"

"That would be my guess."

Thinking the scenario through, I said, "Tina's smaller than him."

"Probably half his weight."

"And Winfrey's about six years younger, too."

"Don't remind me."

I turned to jot a couple of notes down.

"Don't forget he's a professional athlete," Mike said.

"With a bum knee."

"It's not that bad." He clucked his tongue. "He's walking around, going to clubs. He can't steal second base, is all."

"So, the cops are proposing Tina overpowered a younger, bigger man."

"Don't forget he's—"

"What?"

Mike stared at me. "Nothing."

"What?"

His eyes drifted around the room as he searched for an answer. I suspected I knew what he wanted to add, and he was right to keep it to himself.

I closed the notepad and rested my hand on top of it.

"She was scared of him," he said, "because of getting slapped around."

"Uh-huh."

Mike lowered his eyes.

I continued. "Even with the eye test—size and weight—the cops still arrested her. They've got something on her we don't know."

Still looking down, he shrugged. "Doesn't matter."

"How's that?"

"She couldn't have done it. I just know."

"After everything that's occurred?"

Mike lifted his head, and there was the truth I already knew—he still loved her. "All this was my fault."

I cocked my head. "How's that?"

"I took her for granted." He pushed his helmet around with his foot. "Working too much. Going out with the boys. Not paying attention to her. Not paying attention to Jaime." Mike bowed his head again, and his voice softened. "At first, she was my world, but I grew comfortable. Lazy. I should have told her how much I loved her. I did at the beginning—a lot. But after a while, I figured she knew. And I never brought her flowers. You know who did? Winfrey. For no fucking reason, he gave them to her. She told me how much she liked him doing that. Dinner dates or weekend plans, I forgot them. Winfrey didn't." He looked up. "Until recently. When he went back to California."

"That's when she started calling you."

He nodded and wiped some wetness from his face. "Like me, he forgot the most important truth about love."

"Which is?"

"It doesn't last if you're not scared of losing it."

Emotions twisted Mike's face as he fought back the tears. I let him fight his demons and remained silent. When he spoke, it was soft. "Tina's innocent."

"And if you can help prove it, do you think she'll take you back?"

"What if I do?"

"And if I say no?"

Defiantly, he lifted his chin. "I'll do it on my own. I don't need you."

It was false bravado. He was too close to the matter to see straight. If he really wanted to help, the best thing he could was stay out of the way.

Faded memories of Tina Davoli danced in my mind. Family dinners with our little girls running and laughing together in their backyard. Late-night laughs with the three of us sitting around their kitchen table. She was a neat woman, and I knew Mike had taken her for granted.

However, most men did that of their wives or girlfriends. The same could probably be said of most women, too. Familiarity breeds apathy.

Even though she was Tina Winfrey now, I had fond recollections of the woman. I didn't want her sitting in jail without someone in her corner. If I could help, I would, but there would be conditions.

"I'll help," I said, "but we do it my way."

"Yeah, of course."

"And if another bigoted word comes out of your mouth, we're done. Understand?"

Mike's eyes narrowed. "Erika?"

I nodded.

"I didn't know."

"Doesn't matter, but just so we're on the same page—I'll dump you in a hot minute to keep her happy."

"Just like Paige, huh?"

Chapter 6

Years ago, I met Mike for a beer at Kell's Irish Pub near Pike's Street Market. I needed to blow off some steam, and Mike suggested we meet there. A Loudermill hearing was scheduled for the following morning. I faced several disciplinary cases. The hearing would be an opportunity to present my side of the story to the chief of police.

My life seemed to be a hurricane, spiraling faster and faster as it whipped out of control. Mike suggested that Paige McIntyre was in the eye of it all.

A jaunty Irish tune drifted through the bar. It was full of bagpipes and lilting accents. I couldn't make out a word of the song, which irritated me.

"Dump her," Mike said.

"I'm not dumping her."

"She's toxic."

"Stop it."

He eyed me. "Your life's a shitshow since you let her in."

"Not true," I said into my beer.

"Yeah? How about those three charges you got? They happened because of her."

"Two," I said. "One happened before I ever met her."

Mike's eyes narrowed. "Right. The crackhead."

"Crack dealer."

He waved off my comment. "He accused you of stealing from him. He deserves to be called a crackhead. Fuck him."

"Whatever."

"Don't *whatever* me. I'm on your side."

I stared into my beer. No matter how much I talked to it or stared at it, there didn't seem to be any answers there. Yet, I tried to avoid eye contact with Mike. He hadn't liked my girlfriend since I first told him about her several weeks prior. I always knew that he would react poorly. That's why I dated Paige for a couple of months before telling him.

Mike said, "You hit a lieutenant because of her."

We made eye contact now. Mike's disdain for Paige—a woman he had never met—was evident. "She had nothing to do with it. I hit the man because I wanted."

An Internal Affairs lieutenant investigated me due to the crack dealer's accusations. During that process, he discovered my relationship with Paige. There wasn't anything inappropriate there. She danced at The Red Light District, a strip club in downtown Seattle and only a few blocks from where Mike and I had our beers.

During his investigation, the lieutenant tried to get under my skin. He went to the club and hired Paige to dance for him. When that happened, I lost my cool and assaulted the man.

Mike smirked. "Every time I mention her name, you deflect all blame away from her."

"She doesn't have anything to do with anything."

That was true for the third disciplinary charge as well. While in uniform, I assaulted a pimp. My anger had gotten the better of me. It wasn't Paige's fault that I did that. It was my temper and my lack of self-control.

"You must love her."

"What about it?" I snapped.

Mike was pissing me off, and my cheeks warmed. I'd wanted to meet up to get a boost of friendly support.

Instead, he tore down Paige and made me feel like a fool in the process. I couldn't see my face, but it sure as hell felt like I was scowling. For a while, an uncomfortable silence formed between us.

"Well," Mike eventually said, "do you love her?"

"Maybe. I don't know."

He sipped his beer. "You were on a career fast track until she came along."

I barked a cruel laugh, and a nearby table of women looked disapprovingly our way. Mike smiled and nodded at them. I didn't bother with any niceties. They could take their snotty contempt back to Laurelhurst or Madison Park for all I cared.

"Did I strike a nerve?" he asked.

"About the fast track?"

He nodded.

"We're civil service. Union to boot. My career is nothing but time in service and test-taking."

"Reputation matters," Mike said. "Networking, too." He blew a raspberry. "That's all out the window. Your name is for shit, now."

"Said Mike Davoli."

He pulled back, and suspicion clouded his face. "What's that mean?"

"Officer Mopes-A-Lot."

He flicked his beer coaster at me, and it bounced harmlessly against my chest. "Fuck you."

"You already said that."

"No, I said fuck that crackhead. Now, I'm saying fuck you."

"Thanks for the clarification."

More people in the restaurant watched us. A server walked over to check on us. She carried two glasses of water and set them down. We were only on our first beers.

She asked, "How are things going, gentlemen?"

"Fine," I said.

"Fine," Mike parroted.

"Are you ready to order some food?"

Shaking my head, I said, "I'm good."

"Same here."

She put her hand on the table. "Okay. I'll be around if you should change your minds."

When neither of us responded, she wandered away with a furtive glance over her shoulder.

Mike leaned in and whispered, "What's this shit about me moping?"

"You're kidding, right?"

"You'll understand when your wife leaves you for a negro." His head bounced exaggeratedly on the two syllables of the last word.

I rolled my eyes.

Mike leaned in. "I'm trying to save you from a mistake."

"Paige is a mistake?"

"You bet she is."

I smiled, but it wasn't meant to be kind or disarming. It was one of those shitty grins people make when they're about to screw around. My anger boiled, and I felt the perverse need to tip over my friend.

"It's not funny, John."

"It's not? Your wife leaves you, and suddenly you're a relationship expert?"

His face flattened. "You're a real asshole."

"I'm the asshole?"

"That's what I said."

"You're telling me to dump a girlfriend who's been

nothing but good to me because you can't get over a wife getting railed by some other dude."

As he quickly stood, Mike's chair loudly scraped across the floor. The noise in the bar had suddenly dropped and revealed another jaunty Irish tune playing through the speakers. I could hear those lyrics.

In Dublin's fair city
Where the girls are so pretty
I first set my eyes on sweet Molly Malone

Mike angrily pointed at me. "I hope she tears your fucking heart out."

"Not a chance."

"We'll see about that."

He knocked over his chair when he left.

Until he showed up on my doorstep, that was the last time I'd seen or heard from Mike Davoli.

And he was right.

The son of a bitch was actually right.

Paige McIntyre tore out my heart.

Chapter 7

Mike and I stopped at the Kootenai County Jail first. In the lobby, behind a plexiglass shield, sat a heavy-set deputy with a bad combover and a jowly face.

"Tina Winfrey," Mike said and pulled the sign-in clipboard over to him.

The deputy typed something into a nearby computer. "She's unavailable."

"Unavailable?"

"That's what I said."

"The fuck does that mean?"

The clerk frowned, and his jowls became more pronounced. "It means what it means."

Mike turned to me but thumbed at the deputy. "Do you believe this?"

"Next," the clerk said to a couple of women behind us.

Facing the man behind plexiglass again, Mike asked, "What's your name?"

"Deputy."

"The hell?" Mike's cheeks reddened, and he leaned in. He tapped the glass about chest level where the deputy's security tag hung. "I got your name."

"Good for you."

"I'm calling your supervisor."

"Need her number?"

Mike reeled back. "Who the hell—"

I put my hand on Mike's shoulder and pushed him away. "Let me handle this."

He tossed his hands in the air. "Whatever." Mike

walked to the corner of the lobby.

Smiling at the deputy now, a thought whisked through my mind—more flies with honey. "I'm sorry," I said. "My friend is a little emotional. Let's start over. When will Tina Winfrey be available?"

"Later."

"The fuck does that mean?"

***

We next stopped by the Coeur d'Alene Police Department. The officer standing behind the front counter was in her mid-forties with salt and pepper hair. She had bored eyes and a wary smile. Her name tag read *Rascoff*.

After introducing myself, I said, "We'd like to talk with the detective assigned to the Carlton Winfrey murder."

The boredom drained from her eyes. "You have information about the homicide?"

"No, ma'am."

"Then why do you want a detective?"

"We're friends of the woman arrested."

Rascoff's eyes flicked to Mike, then returned to me. "Friends?"

"Yes, ma'am."

"And you want access to a major crimes detective?"

The way she asked the question—full of disbelief—made me feel stupid. No detective would speak with us if we didn't have beneficial information. We were delusional even to think so. Maybe an investigator would take our name and number and give us a polite runaround—something about contact if they needed additional background—but that wouldn't help Tina today.

Thank God we hadn't made it worse by announcing that

I was a private investigator or Mike was her ex-husband. The best thing we could do was to apologize for inconveniencing the front desk officer and leave.

The woman bent slightly forward as if to encourage an answer.

I cleared my throat. "I'm sorry for—"

"I'm her ex-husband," Mike interrupted. He lifted his hand to his chest in the sincerest gesture he could muster.

Rascoff frowned. "Of the woman they arrested?"

Mike glanced at me, and I shook my head.

"Weren't you already questioned?" the duty officer asked.

He turned back to her. "Yeah, but they didn't find any reason to suspect me."

In hopes of aborting this mission, I touched Mike's arm. Not seeing the danger, he pulled his arm away.

"I'm a cop," he said with more bravado than necessary. Motioning toward me, Mike added, "And he used to be."

"Is that so?" She judged us the way experienced cops do. "You're out of your jurisdiction, so that and three bucks will get you a cup of coffee."

Mike's brow furrowed. "But we think she's innocent."

"You *think*?"

His face hardened. "We *know*."

"Oh, well, since you know." The officer eyed me as she grabbed her pen. "The detectives are busy right now. Give me your names and numbers, and I'll have them call you."

***

"A waste of time," Mike said, then slammed his door shut.

"No, it wasn't."

I started the truck and dropped it into gear.

"How do you figure?" he asked.

"We know what not to do next time."

"Mr. Positive Attitude. When did that happen?"

I stopped at the exit of the police department's parking lot. "Do you know where Winfrey lived?"

"Yeah."

He pointed left, and I bounced the truck into the street. Mike reached for the dash as he didn't have a seatbelt on.

"It's still a crime scene," Mike said.

"I want to see where it went down. Maybe wrap my brain around it. We're not going to break in."

We traveled for a bit with him occasionally pointing left and right. We made a wrong turn early on, but he realized it and turned us around before we wasted too much time. When we made it to Northwest Boulevard, things hummed along. We drove through downtown and along the lake. Cute neighborhoods abutted our path. Sun glinted off the water. Near the water's edge were several marinas, and boats motored toward the center of the lake.

The whole scene—the massive watercraft, the fancy cars, and even the beautiful people milling about—exuded money. Coeur d'Alene might be a tourist town, but it's loaded with luxury.

"Almost there," Mike said. "It's on Merchant Road." He pointed ahead. "Turn here."

The road leading to Carlton Winfrey's place was winding and tight. It leveled off a quarter of a mile up and opened onto a straightaway that ended in a cul-de-sac. The homes were large with small lawns. Expensive cars were in the driveways. To the east was a spectacular view of the lake. If the initial impression was to make a visitor feel envious, the neighborhood was doing a fine job.

It wasn't difficult to guess which house belonged to Carlton Winfrey. A patrol cruiser sat in front of a white two-level with brown trim. Yellow police tape surrounded the property line. In its driveway was a shiny black Humvee and a red Jaguar.

Mike lifted his chin toward the house. "The Hummer is Winfrey's. The Jag belongs to Tina."

"Did they drive them up?"

"His boys did."

As we passed the patrol car decorated with the Coeur d'Alene Police Department logo, the officer leaned over to get a better look at us. I waved and smiled.

We finished circling the cul-de-sac and headed out of the neighborhood,

Mike cocked his head to check his rearview mirror. "Guy is probably running your plate."

"If he's doing his job."

In the rearview mirror, I watched the cop car. The driver's door opened, and the officer got out. He was an older man with a beer belly. A blue baseball cap sat pushed back on his head. He lifted his arms to stretch, then leaned from side to side.

"Somehow," I said, "I don't think he's worried about running anything."

Still watching his mirror, Mike agreed. "Retired on duty. We probably could have walked through the house, and the guy wouldn't have made a peep."

Chapter 8

Erika and I sat in one of the booths at The Elk, a small bistro in the middle of the Browne's Addition neighborhood. Hipster music played through the radio.

"Where's your friend?" she asked finally.

"I don't know."

Up until now, we'd made small talk about her school, how much she liked the restaurant, and if I was ready to bounce this upcoming weekend. She'd taken her time getting to the subject of Mike Davoli. Now, we were there.

"Are you going to help him?"

"I'm not helping *him*."

Her eyes narrowed.

"I'm helping his ex-wife. She's the one in jail."

Erika's face relaxed, then she briefly looked away. After sipping her drink, she asked, "Is this a paying job?"

"Probably not."

"Should be."

I couldn't think of a reason to disagree, so I stayed silent.

The waitress walked over with two plates in her hands. "Here you go." She placed a grilled chicken pita in front of me. She set a plate of lamb tacos in front of Erika.

As the server left, Erika said, "Thanks for taking me out."

"Of course."

She bit into a taco, moaned in culinary pleasure, and began chewing.

I asked, "What happened this morning between you and

Mike?"

Her chewing slowed, and she set down the taco. "Well," she said, then wiped her hands. "He was surprised to see me."

"I hadn't told him about you."

"It wasn't that."

I pulled my beer close and held it, waiting for her concerns.

"I've seen that look before."

"You're an attractive woman. He was probably—"

"I'm black," she said. It was a statement, and a challenge rolled together. When I didn't reply, she continued. "He was surprised to see me in your house. It wasn't the hateful way some look at me, but what I saw was in the same family."

I lowered my eyes.

"When your friend spoke, something was missing in his voice. You know how you talk with friends? Happy. Maybe relaxed. And when you meet a person you know is connected to that friend, you'll usually talk in the same manner. We all do it. But not him. It was as if he was talking to someone less."

"I'm sorry."

"You knew about it?"

"He wasn't always like that."

"But you knew. That's why you avoided the subject of him when I asked."

"Yeah."

She pushed her plate away. "So, if he wasn't always like this, what happened to him—this friend of yours? Why did he change?"

"His wife left."

Erika closed her eyes and tilted her head back as if in

thought. "The ballplayer, right? The wife left him for a ballplayer." When she looked at me again, Erika said, "The guy's black."

"Uh-huh."

"I don't buy it."

"What's to buy?"

"That your friend becomes a racist because of that. He was a racist before."

I shook my head.

"Racism isn't a flower, John. It doesn't bloom overnight."

"I don't know. He never said anything racist before."

"Maybe not overtly," she said, "but how about a little joke here or there? Or the odd comment that everyone waved off as being 'just Mike.' Any of that sound familiar?"

It sounded like a lot of guys actually—maybe even me. I couldn't remember ever making comments about skin color, but I knew I had made plenty of jokes and snide remarks about gender, sexual preference, or mental capacity. Shame warmed my face. The run-in with Terry Newsome played in my mind, and the crowd of laughing men bothered me.

"Let's drop it," she said and pulled her plate closer again. "I'm hungry."

After that, we finished our meals mostly in silence. When the waitress took our plates, we sipped what remained of our drinks.

"What do you think?" Erika asked.

"I thought it was good."

"Not your sandwich. The murder. Do you think the ex-wife did it?"

"Her name is Tina." I folded my arms. "And I have no

idea."

"What if Tina really did it?"

"For me, nothing."

"And your friend?"

I shrugged.

"Is this guy worth it?"

"I'm not doing it for him."

"You said that. You're doing it for her. Is that how you're justifying your involvement?"

"Tina was a nice woman. If no one is in her corner—"

"She'll have an attorney. She's not alone."

"You know what I mean."

Erika stared into her glass. "Does your friend have a problem with us?"

"Why would he?"

"He's a racist."

"I already told you he wasn't."

"And I told you he was. Believe me—I'm the one with the dark skin."

I inhaled deeply and puffed out my cheeks. "Listen. I do believe you, but I'm sure he doesn't have a problem with us."

"You're sure?"

I nodded.

"Why do you think that is?"

Was I ready to admit that I loved her? I didn't have to admit it to Mike, but he sensed it—knew it—by how I talked about Erika. Did I want to tell her something that important in a moment like this? Hell no, I decided. This was an ugly moment. Better to stay silent and be thought a fool.

"I'll tell you why he doesn't have a problem," Erika said. "It's because you're a white man, and I'm a black woman."

"That's not why."

"It's been like that since the plantations." She slid out of the booth. "Thank you for dinner."

"You're leaving?"

"I've got homework." Standing by the table now, she glanced around the restaurant. "If I asked you not to help your friend—"

"I'm not—"

She faced me. "You *are*."

I kept quiet.

"If I asked you not to, would you?"

"In a heartbeat."

Her smile was soft and didn't hide her hurt. "Call me tomorrow." She turned and left.

I sat alone in the restaurant, waiting for the server to return with the bill.

Chapter 9

The following day, Mike and I met in the parking lot of the Kootenai County Jail. Standing with Mike was a lanky guy in a sharp blue suit. He sported a thirty-dollar haircut, flawless skin, and perfect teeth. His left hand clutched a scuffed leather briefcase.

"John," Mike said, "This is Butch Hollingshead, Tina's attorney."

Butch seemed a name reserved for rednecks, unleashed dogs, or dirty-faced boys in black and white movies. I kept my thoughts to myself and shook hands with the attorney.

"What's their evidence?" I asked.

"Right to business," Butch said with an effortless smile.

The dinner with Erika had soured me on helping Mike and Tina. Erika hadn't returned my repeated phone calls. Had I not feared putting our drama on display in front of her parents, I would have driven over to her house.

I should have canceled when I got Mike's message about meeting the lawyer. He could figure this situation out on his own. He didn't need me. And Tina could hire someone else to help. As Erika pointed out, I wasn't getting paid to create drama in our relationship.

Butch walked over to a silver BMW. He casually flopped the briefcase on the trunk and popped it open. "I'm sharing this information with you," he reached into the bag, "because Mrs. Winfrey advised that you are on retainer as a private investigator."

"I'm not on retainer."

Butch paused with his hand still in the briefcase. "Then

what *are* you?"

"A friend."

"He's an advisor," Mike said. He patted my shoulder. "John's an advisor."

The attorney considered Mike's words, then handed me a business card. "Stop by the office. We'll need some paperwork so we can get you paid. Identify your hourly rate, acceptable expenses, and whatnot."

I studied the card while Butch continued.

"Mrs. Winfrey informed me that I could share any information with the both of you." He pulled a notepad from the briefcase. "The police and the prosecuting attorney have not turned anything over yet. They're still building their case, but here's what we know." He consulted his yellow pad. "Someone stabbed Carlton Winfrey. He was found clothed in bed."

"Single wound?" I asked.

Butch nodded. "Right in the chest."

"That would take some force."

The attorney consulted his pad again.

I continued. "Lucky they didn't break the knife. Was the strike made downward?" I mimed the motion. "As in, Winfrey was already on the bed when he was killed. Or was it a thrusting attack, and Winfrey fell backward onto the bed?"

Butch shrugged. "Investigators haven't confirmed one way or another. The medical examiner hasn't finished their report."

"Defensive wounds?"

"Doesn't appear to be any."

That seemed odd. Could the one knife strike have rendered Winfrey immediately incapacitated? A killing blow. Or did the killer strike Winfrey and then hold him down? That would require more strength than Tina likely had. Were there two killers then?

Butch said, "They don't suspect sexual intercourse before the murder."

"But they're checking?" I asked.

"Of course. The investigators did find a knife in a cutlery block. It was clean but appeared to match the wound size on Mr. Winfrey. It's been sent out for testing to see if there is any blood residue."

"Any other evidence?" I asked.

"Blood spatter on the bathroom floor. No blood elsewhere in the house."

"Killer washed their hands?"

"Likely."

"Forced entry?"

Butch shook his head.

"And Tina called the police?"

"That's correct."

I ran the facts through my head once more to make sure I understood them. Then I said, "How can they charge Tina? They don't have enough hard evidence to point at her. What am I missing?"

Mike simply nodded.

Butch tossed the notepad into the briefcase and shut it. "Tina lied."

"Lied?" Mike and I said in unison.

"A neighbor saw Tina's car in the driveway that morning."

"So?" Mike blurted. He was finally engaged in the conversation

"Tina told the investigators she was at the gym during the murder. She arrived home and found her husband murdered."

Mike pointed. "So, it's the witness that jammed Tina up?"

Butch shook his head. "Tina did it to herself."

I glanced at Mike, who watched the attorney with rapt attention.

"Tina's a member of a fitness club where everyone signs in and out by swiping a card." Butch mimicked the action. "Therefore, each visit is recorded."

"Maybe," Mike said, "she forgot to check-in. That can happen. Right?"

"No, it can't. The door is locked. Outside of regular hours, which Tina claimed the visit was, a member must use the keycard to get inside. So, you see the problem."

Mike's face pinched, and he looked away.

"They caught her in a lie," I said. "People get nervous."

Butch nodded. "I agree. It happens, and it's not the end of the world." Using a fob, he opened the trunk to the BMW and tossed the briefcase inside. "But when the police told her about the lie, she changed her story."

"To what?" Mike asked.

Butch eyed him.

"*What?*"

"She said she met you for breakfast."

Mike's head snapped to me, then back to the attorney.

Butch continued. "But you told the cops you had breakfast at your hotel."

"No, no," Mike said quickly. "She met me."

"Don't." Butch shook his head. "Just don't. It won't help, and it'll also get you into trouble. Besides, staff members confirmed you ate alone."

I asked, "Did the cops point out they knew the second lie?"

"Not before giving Tina enough rope to hang herself."

"Jesus," Mike said.

"Tina tried to explain away her first lie by saying she didn't want Carlton's entourage to find out she was meeting her ex-husband. Supposedly, she's afraid of them."

"That's no bullshit," Mike said. "I can verify that. I will verify that."

"Regardless," Butch continued, "she intimated a romantic rendezvous with you."

Mike's ears reddened.

"Her story falls apart because of the neighbor seeing her car, your statement, and the hotel staff's testimony. The cops had all that information before she started lying. The investigators let her put her head into the noose before they tugged it tight. When they did, she stopped talking and demanded a lawyer. That's when I came in."

Mike and I exchanged looks.

"Did she ever say where she was?" Mike asked.

"No," Butch said. "She wouldn't tell me either. I tried to advise her that it was in her best interest, but she's remaining tight-lipped about it."

I shoved my hands into my pockets. "What are the cops saying motivated Tina to kill her husband?"

"Divorce."

"Divorce?" Mike parroted.

I said, "Murder is a harsh way to end a marriage."

The attorney's smile was humorless. "The investigators found divorce papers in the kitchen. Tina claims she never saw them, but the cops have them in evidence."

"Hold up." Mike waved his hands. "*Winfrey* wanted a divorce?"

Butch nodded. "According to the police, he was the requesting party. I have not seen copies of the papers yet."

"So that we're all on the same page," I said, "let's run this whole thing back. This is how the cops say this thing went down. Carlton Winfrey wanted a divorce. Somehow Tina discovered the paperwork and went into the kitchen with it. She became so enraged by the news of the pending separation that she took a knife from the cutlery block."

Mike and Butch watched as I continued to assemble the pieces of Tina's prosecution.

"Then she found Winfrey in the bedroom and stabbed him. Afterward, she cleaned up, returned the knife to where she found it and called the police to say, 'Help, help, someone murdered my husband.'"

The attorney said, "That sounds about right."

Mike shuffled from foot to foot and shook his head. "Oh, man," he muttered. "Oh, man."

"It's too simple," I said.

The attorney cocked his head.

"She flies off the handle, stabs the guy, then calls the cops."

Butch put his hand on the back of the car. "Listen. I'm not saying she did any of it, but a lot of crimes are as simple as that."

Mike stepped forward. "If Winfrey was going to divorce Tina, why wouldn't she tell me? She'd tell me. I know it."

The attorney waved dismissively. "She didn't know."

Maybe she did know and was embarrassed to tell Mike. It seemed farfetched, but stranger things have happened. Tina had left Mike to be with Carlton Winfrey. Admitting to Mike that Winfrey wanted to leave her might be humiliating. She probably would have told her attorney about the impending divorce, although there was something else that she refused to reveal.

"The big question," I said, "is if she wasn't at that house that morning, then where was she?"

Butch's expression flattened. "Your guess is as good as mine. She won't say."

Mike said, "Tina and I met for breakfast together."

"Lying under oath is a crime, Officer Davoli."

"Will Tina see us?" I asked.

"You are part of the defense team, but since you're not an attorney and you're not family, you have to go in one at a time. I'll start preparing for the first appearance hearing."

"Will bail happen?" Mike asked, hope evident in his eyes.

"It's unlikely, but I'll still make a run at it."

Butch walked around to the driver's door of the BMW. Mike and I stepped away from the car. Without a word of goodbye, the attorney dropped inside.

We headed toward the jail.

***

While Mike talked with Tina, I waited in the lobby.

The waiting room's linoleum flooring was scuffed and scarred. Hard plastic chairs were bolted to steel bars which were secured to the floor. Overhead fluorescent lighting buzzed like hundreds of crazed flies.

Two teenage blond girls sat nearby. Huddled, one of them openly sobbed while the other tried to comfort her.

Across the way, a nattily dressed mid-fifties white man rested the back of his head against the wall. His eyes were closed as he spoke softly into his cell phone. He gestured with his free hand while he talked.

Heavy emotions descended over the entire jail. It was as if all humanity's negative emotions had permeated the concrete walls. On the other side, anger, fear, and loneliness thrived. Inside the lobby lived sadness, disappointment, and anxiety.

All jails felt this way. I'd been to several now. None were happy places.

Thirty minutes after he went in, Mike came out. His eyes were red, and his head hung in defeat. He dropped onto the plastic chair next to me.

"Everything okay?" I asked.

He shrugged.

"We'll get her out." I tried to sound convincing.

***

Tina Winfrey's eyes met mine as soon as I stepped into the visiting room. She sat at the opposite wall.

Detainees and visitors were separated by a low barrier that ran the room's length. On both sides of the wall was a counter. Every few feet were small dividers to give the appearance of privacy, but voices easily carried.

A guard stood inside the room to monitor the prisoners.

I sat across from Tina.

She wore an orange jumpsuit that hung loosely from her shoulders. Light bruising was visible under her left eye, a tell-tale piece of evidence of Carlton's earlier domestic assault. Were the cops using this as part of her motivation for killing her husband? She hadn't reported it, so maybe they didn't know.

"How're you holding up?" I asked.

"Fine." She glanced back toward the guard. "I feel like I'm in an episode of *The Twilight Zone*."

"I'll bet." I pulled out my notebook and pen.

"Mike said you quit the police department."

I hadn't seen Tina in years, and she was trying to reconnect. Jumping into the questions surrounding her husband's death wasn't the smart thing to do. She wanted to build some rapport. We needed to build trust. "I left a couple years back."

"Over a girl, right?"

"It's more complicated than that."

"With you?" She smiled. "I can imagine. So, you're a private investigator now?"

"Licensed even."

"Does it pay well?"

"Not yet."

"How do you make ends meet?" It was small talk, but maybe that allowed her a sense of normalcy. "Have you got a trust fund somewhere?"

"I work the door at a nightclub."

"A bouncer?" she asked. "Where at?"

"Club Royale. It's in Spokane."

"I've heard of that place. It's like *the* club, isn't it?"

"For now. Clubs come and go."

"Carlton's boys go there sometimes."

"They do?" Not knowing what they look like, they might have passed me many times inside the club.

She nodded. "How's Erin?"

"Good. She just stayed with me."

Her face brightened. In the orange jumpsuit, the smile seemed out of place. "She's got to be thirteen now."

"Right."

"Same age as Jaime. I bet she's pretty."

"A heartbreaker."

Tina glanced back at the guard. "Mike said you could help figure this thing out."

"If you lay out the truth. Not the bullshit you're

shoveling for everyone else."

"I told the truth."

"Then you'll go to prison."

Tina's eyes hardened.

"If you don't feel like telling the truth, it's no skin off my nose."

"What about Mike?"

"I'm not here for him. I'm here for you, but if you don't want to tell the truth, I don't need friends like that."

"You've gotten cold, John."

I shrugged. "The cops have you boxed in with two lies. First, you said you went to the gym, and then you said you met Mike for breakfast. The cops disproved both. That idiot in the lobby would happily corroborate your second lie and jam himself up. But not me. I'm not here for that. Either tell me the truth, or I walk."

"No skin off your nose."

I put my pen on the notepad and folded my arms. "I'm not the one behind bars."

Tina leaned back in her chair, and the front legs came off the floor.

"Four on the floor," the guard ordered.

Every head turned in his direction, and she dropped her chair back into position. Tina said, "Sorry."

"Keep it on the ground," the guard muttered.

When her gaze returned to me, Tina said, "I was with someone."

"Doing what?"

She cocked her head and bulged her eyes.

"Really?"

"Carlton was doing it. Why couldn't I?"

"What's his name?"

"Rembrandt Easton."

I wrote the name. "What kind of name is that?"

"He's an artist."

"Is that his given name?"

"He legally changed it when he turned eighteen."

"How'd you meet him?"

"At an art show."

"In Los Angeles?"

"Where else?"

"What's he doing up here?"

Another head tilt and more bulging eyes.

"How long has he been here?"

"About three weeks."

"How long have you been seeing this guy?"

"I don't know, maybe two months."

"Is it serious?"

Tina shrugged. "We pretend it is, but he knows I'm married and that I wasn't planning on leaving my husband."

"Why wouldn't you leave?"

"It's complicated."

"Uncomplicate it."

"Comfort is a tough thing to walk away from." She rubbed her hands together. "I had a good life. My daughter had a good home. We could go anywhere, do anything, and buy anything we wanted. That's heady stuff when a person gets indoctrinated into it. At first, I thought Carlton's spending was a waste of money, but after a while, I found myself living the lifestyle and getting used to it."

"You didn't stay for love?"

"Love dies. People either leave when it does, or they find another reason to stay. Mine was comfort."

"Sounds mercenary."

"Says the man who's never been married." Her face

immediately softened. "I'm sorry, John. That was uncalled for."

I lifted a hand for her to stop. "It's fine. You're right. I don't know. This Rembrandt—what's he do for a living?"

"I told you. He's an artist."

"What kind of art?"

"He paints. Plays the guitar. Writes poetry."

I wanted to laugh. "That pays the rent?"

"He tends bar when he has to."

"Three weeks is a lot of time to be away from a job."

"He's not working right now."

"Are you supporting him?"

"He's his own man." She sounded defensive.

"That didn't answer my question."

She looked away. "I help out when he needs it, but it's because I want to, not because he needs it."

"Uh-huh. Where can I find this guy?"

Her eyes widened. "Why?"

"So that I can verify your story."

"You're not going to hurt him?"

"Why would I hurt him?"

Tina studied me for a moment before saying, "The resort."

"That's a nice place. What room?"

She told me.

"How did you hide that expense from Carlton? You're not working either."

"I had an allowance."

"That was nice of your husband."

Her face soured. "I earned every penny of it."

"Sounds like you did a good job."

"Don't be a pig."

"I'm not. I'm trying to understand how you could afford

to stash a boyfriend at the resort."

Tina looked away. "It was my rainy-day fund."

"Why haven't you come forward about Rembrandt?"

"He's had some troubles."

"What kind of troubles can an artist have?"

Tina glanced back at the guard. "He ran drugs when he was a teenager, but he's over that now."

"Who cares if he ran drugs?"

"When he was a kid," she whispered, "he shot a man. Did time for it."

"In juvenile?"

"That's why I don't want the cops looking at him."

I briefly looked away, and a thought came to me. "Carlton was stabbed in bed."

"If he hooked up with someone, it wasn't me."

"Who was it then?"

"How would I know? Carlton had his side pieces, and I had mine."

"Did he know about Rembrandt?"

She pointed at the bruising around her eye. "He suspected."

"How long had he been hitting you?"

"A while. When things got bad, he tended to lash out at those around him. When he suspected I had someone, he'd put me back in line."

"How often did you have someone on the side?"

"A few times, but it was nothing compared to what he was doing."

"Did he ever hit Jaime?"

"No. And he never hit me in front of her. He yelled. Maybe threw some things, but hit me? No. He saved that for when we were alone, and it wasn't as often as I'm making it sound."

"Did you ever report it?"

"No."

"Why not?"

"I already told you—comfort is a bitch. Besides, things seemed to be going better for a while. Then the injury happened, and the rehab started. It all seemed too much for him."

"Did his crew know about the hitting?"

She nodded.

"Have they talked to the cops?"

"I don't know. Why?"

I waved off her question. Yet, that could be a damning piece of witness testimony in the hands of a prosecutor. It went to motive. Tina Winfrey killed her husband because he repeatedly assaulted her.

"Could Rembrandt have killed Carlton?"

"No way. Not a chance."

"What about Carlton's friends? Could any of them have killed him?"

"I doubt it. They were loyal. And he was loyal to them, too. It was a strange bond. Like, once a fan got crazy around Carlton, and the boys beat the holy hell out of the guy. But another time, when Carlton got angry at me, a couple of them eyed him like a pit bull would a wounded rabbit."

"What are their names?"

"Bone, Grouch, Squirrel, and Bumps."

"Their *real* names."

She told me, and I jotted the information into my notebook.

"What will they do now that Carlton's dead? Are they going to head home to LA?"

Tina looked up at the ceiling. "If I had to guess, I'd say

no. At least, not right away. They were his entourage, and Carlton paid for everything. He even bought them a couple black Escalades to travel in style."

She was quiet while I wrote a note about the vehicles. When I looked up, she continued.

"They're going to want to blame someone for Carlton's murder, and they're going to want some revenge. Maybe they already blame me. If they find out about Rembrandt, they'll kill him. It'll be out of some warped sense of honor. Being in here might be the safest place to be until the real killer is found."

"Is there anything else you want to tell me about Rembrandt? Doesn't seem enough of a reason to keep his existence a secret."

She let out a long, slow sigh. When she was finished, she whispered, "He's got a warrant."

"For?"

"Robbery."

I leaned in and whispered, "Are you kidding me?"

"It's total bullshit."

"Robbery is a felony. It's not bullshit."

"He broke into an art gallery to steal back one of his paintings."

"Sounds like burglary, not robbery."

"He might have fought with the gallery's owner."

The guard seemed interested in our conversation, so I lowered my voice further. "What kind of guy are you messing with?"

"It's all a mistake," she said.

"Cops don't make mistakes like that."

"If that's true, why am I here?"

I closed my notebook. "It's not the same."

"How do you know?"

I wanted to say because she was my friend, but at that moment I realized I didn't know the woman any longer. Pushing back my chair, I stood. "I'll be in touch." Without waiting for her to respond, I headed for the door.

"How do you know?" she shouted.

Chapter 10

"She *what*?" Mike's voice spiked with anger.

"Relax."

"Fuck you. You relax."

We were seated inside my truck with the engine running and the air conditioning blowing. My notebook lay open on my leg.

"She's lying again," Mike said.

"Not this time." I closed the notebook and tucked it between my legs.

He punched the dash. "Why didn't she tell me?"

"Because she knew you'd react this way."

Mike punched the dash twice more.

"And you say I have anger issues."

He glared at me.

I slipped my seatbelt on, then dropped the truck into gear. Mike didn't bother securing his safety belt.

"Why would she do that?" he asked.

"She probably needed someone."

"But she could have come back." He sounded like a whiny teenager. "I would have let her."

The Ford bounced as we left the parking lot. "That's not how things work."

"She can kiss my ass if she thinks I'm helping now."

"That's how you want to play it?"

"Damn right, that's how I want to play it. She gets what she gets. The bitch laid down with dogs. Let her get some fleas."

"Now, she's a bitch?"

Mike didn't answer and simply stared straight ahead. At the next stoplight, I studied him. His eyes were filled with jealousy, and his cheeks were flushed.

He punched the dash again. "I would have done anything—anything—to get her back."

"Then do it now."

"Light's green."

The truck lurched forward. After we cleared the intersection, I changed lanes.

"You're full of shit, Mike."

"What are you talking about?"

"You come to me with a load of crap. Saying you still love her. Saying you want to win her back. You don't love her."

He faced me.

"You only want her back because she left you."

Mike's voice lowered as his anger bubbled back to life. "You don't know shit."

"This is about your ego."

He flipped the bird. "Suck my dick."

I mashed the brakes, and the truck skidded to an abrupt halt in the middle of the road. Not wearing his seatbelt, Mike slipped from the seat, fell to the floorboard, and hit the side of his head against the dash. I accelerated out of traffic to the side of the road and popped the truck into Park.

"Now, listen—" I said.

Mike jumped from the floorboard. I held up a hand to stop him, but he knocked it down. He threw a punch that landed squarely on my forehead. My head whipped back and hit the driver's door window.

"Ow!" he yelled. Mike spun and angrily tried to open the door three times before succeeding. He leaped from the truck and walked several feet away. He alternated between shaking and cradling his hand.

When there was a break in traffic, I climbed out and walked around to the shoulder. Vehicles whizzed by as the two of us stared at each other.

I asked, "Did you break your hand?"

"I don't think so." He rubbed his knuckles.

"You're out of control."

"I'm fine."

"Remember how I was with Paige? Wild and mean. Ready to tear the head off the world. That's how you are."

Mike looked away, and a car honked as it sped by.

I said, "You're an asshole."

"Probably."

"No probably about it. I'm telling you so you can get yourself in check."

He licked his lips. "If you want, I can walk back to my hotel. It can't be more than a mile."

I waved him toward the truck. "Get in."

Mike fastened his seatbelt this time, and I merged the truck merged into traffic. We continued toward the resort. We rode in silence for a couple of minutes.

"What's his name again?" Mike asked.

"Rembrandt."

"Figures."

"How so?"

"Never mind." He looked out the window. "Why don't we just turn this turd over to the cops and get her out?"

"Tina doesn't want that, so let's try to do it her way."

"Whatever." He didn't look at me, but it was clear he was sulking.

"If we can't make heads or tails of it, we'll talk about turning him over. Okay?"

Several minutes later, we skipped the resort's parking garage and found a spot along Sherman Avenue. I wriggled the truck into the parking stall and turned it off.

Mike popped open his door.

"Wait here," I said and climbed out.

When he walked around the front of the truck, he spread his arms out. "Why do I have to wait outside?"

"Because we don't need two guys to talk with him."

"You need back-up. I've seen how you fight." Mike patted my shoulder as he headed toward the building. "What room is this piece of squeeze in?"

***

Mike slowed when he entered the hotel. "Nice."

The Coeur d'Alene Resort overlooks the lake, which teems with activity during the summer months. Visitors swarm the sandy beaches, less than a block away, when the sun comes up. Expensive boats dock at the nearby marina—those with less disposable income dock their craft further down the lake. There are restaurants on the first and seventh floors which bring in the day visitors.

Both Mike and I were underdressed for the hotel. He wore khaki cargo pants, a black polo shirt, and combat boots. I wore faded Levi's, a black t-shirt, and Doc Martens. Compared to the resort's patrons, we looked out of place—two dayworkers among a mass of vacationers.

As we passed the lobby's welcome desk, a pasty-faced clerk popped up from his chair like a groundhog sensing danger. He watched with suspicion as we headed toward the elevators.

"Can I help you, gentlemen?" The clerk scurried around the desk.

"We're good," I said and waved. Mike and I stepped into a waiting elevator.

I pressed the button for the eleventh floor. When the doors closed, Mike and I leaned against opposite walls. The illuminated numbers above the door changed as we ascended.

"Why do I feel like we're burglarizing the joint?" he asked.

"That's how the hotel wants us to feel."

He raised an eyebrow.

"It's not special if it feels like we can afford it. Exclusivity as marketing."

"You are such a democrat."

I rolled my eyes.

"So," Mike said, "what's this Rembrandt guy do that he can afford to stay in a place like this?"

I shrugged. "Who knows?"

If Mike was pissed that Tina saw Rembrandt on the side, he would tip over to learn she was paying his way.

When the elevator doors opened, we stepped into the eleventh-floor hallway.

"When we get there," I said, "let me do the talking."

Mike opened his mouth to say something but thought better of it.

Outside the hotel room, I stepped to one side of the door. Mike moved to the other. Just like old times. I knocked twice.

"Yeah?" a voice lazily called from inside.

"Maintenance," I said.

"I didn't call."

"We need to come inside, sir."

"For what?"

"There's a plumbing problem." Mike pointed to the

sky, so I added, "In the room above."

The guy said, "I don't see anything."

"Sir, we need to come in and verify no damage."

Mike nodded his approval at my ruse.

"Yeah, okay," the guy inside the room responded. "Whatever."

A moment later, the lock turned, and the door cracked open. He was in his early thirties with blue eyes and long, wavy brown hair. He eyed me skeptically. Mike was up against the opposite wall, out of the occupant's line of sight. Neither of them could see the other.

"You don't look like maintenance," Blue Eyes said.

"I'm with the contractor. We need to verify no water damage." I pointed upward to emphasize my point. "We'll be in and out."

"Fine. Do it fast." Blue Eyes stepped back and pulled the door open. He wore only a pair of boxer shorts. He was tall, lean, and handsome.

I stepped into the room and tried to block the way, but Mike slipped by me—a single bull running through the streets of Pamplona.

Blue Eyes stiffened. "Hey. What is this?"

"He's white." Mike sounded baffled and stalked toward the room's occupant.

I grabbed Mike's shoulder and yanked him back.

"The hell?" he said.

"This isn't helping."

Mike yanked free of my grasp, which caused the lean man to jump. He stumbled backward, tripped over himself, and fell onto the carpet. Blue Eyes crab-walked toward the center of the room.

"We're here for Tina," I said to Mike. "Not you."

Blue Eyes quit moving and dropped to his butt. "Tina?"

Mike jitterbugged around my extended arm. "But he's white."

"No shit," Blue Eyes said. "So are you." His eyes narrowed. "Are you cops?"

I pointed to the piece of furniture in the corner. "Mike, check the chair." To Rembrandt, I said. "We're private investigators working for Tina."

Mike stood frozen over Rembrandt. Confusion played out on his face. I snapped my fingers in front of Mike's eyes to break his trance. When he looked at me, I said, "The chair."

He lumbered toward the wingback and lifted the seat cushion. Finding nothing, he shoved the pad back into place. "Clear."

"Get up," I told Rembrandt, "and sit there."

The guy scooted across the floor before climbing into the chair. "What do you want?"

"Some answers."

Rembrandt eyed Mike. "Is he okay?"

Mike scowled. "What kind of fucking name is Rembrandt?"

Defensively, Rembrandt said, "It's a perfectly acceptable name."

"Not for a white guy."

I opened my hands in a what-are-you-doing gesture to Mike. He ignored me.

"What's your problem?" Rembrandt asked.

Mike lifted a single finger. "Name one other guy with that name."

"Rembrandt Harmenszoon van Rijn."

"Who?"

"The painter."

Mike lifted a second finger. "Besides him."

"Rembrandt Bugatti."

"The motorcycle?"

"The sculptor."

Mike grunted and crossed his arms. His scowl deepened as he watched the room's occupant.

Rembrandt turned back to me. "Does he have low blood sugar or something?"

"Or something," I said. "Are you aware that Tina's in jail?"

"For real?"

"I'll take that as a no."

"What happened?"

"The cops think she killed her husband."

"No way." Rembrandt waved his hands as if he were putting out a fire. "Not Tina."

"Because she loved Carlton?"

His laugh was polite. "That's funny."

Mike's mocking laugh was not polite. "No. That is not funny."

Rembrandt glanced sideways at Mike. "Who are you?"

"I'm her husband."

"No, you're not. Carlton Is. Was." Rembrandt snapped his fingers. "You're the cop."

"And how do you know that?"

"Tina told me about her ex."

Mike scowled and pushed off the wall. "Care to share?"

Rembrandt turned away from him. "Why are you guys in my room?"

"We're trying to prove Tina's innocence, and you're the guy that can help."

His eyes widened. "Wait. You don't mean you want me to talk with the cops."

"That's exactly what we mean," Mike said. He moved

toward Rembrandt. I put my hand out to hold him back, but he swatted it away. "I don't know what she saw in you, little man—"

"Little man?" Rembrandt muttered, but he didn't try to come out of his chair.

Mike continued. "—but you're going to speak up for her. And if you don't, I'll drag your faggotty ass down to the police station." When he reached for Rembrandt, I pushed Mike away.

"What is your problem?" he asked.

"Wait in the truck."

"I'm not waiting outside."

"Yeah," Rembrandt said, "wait outside so the adults can talk."

Mike pointed at Rembrandt. "Watch yourself."

"Please," I said. "Let me talk with him."

Mike's gaze darted between Rembrandt and me. "Whatever." He turned to leave.

"Thank you."

"That's impressive," Rembrandt said. "Now, can you teach him to fetch?"

Mike lunged for the man and punched Rembrandt in the chest. I hooked Mike's arm as he reared back for a second strike and yanked him off the artist. With a spin, I tossed Mike to the floor.

"Go outside!" I yelled.

Slowly rising from the ground, Mike pointed at Rembrandt. "I owe you, smart ass."

Rembrandt rubbed his chest. "Tough guy."

"I should kick your ass, too," Mike said to me. "Protecting that piece of shit."

"Go outside. *Now.*"

"Tina doesn't love him."

"More than you," Rembrandt said.

Mike lunged again, but I caught him and spun him around this time. With a two-handed shove, I propelled him toward the door. He didn't look back before leaving.

We waited for the door to click shut before continuing.

"Your friend has anger management issues," Rembrandt said.

Most people say that about me. I was starting to look calm with Mike around.

I motioned at his boxers. "Put some pants on."

Rembrandt collected a pair of jeans and slid into them. When he buttoned the fly, he flopped back into the chair and ran his fingers through his longish hair. "So, Tina's in jail?"

"That's right."

"Explains why she hasn't contacted me."

"And you haven't tried to reach out to her?"

He smirked. "That's not how this works. I wait for her. That's the safest. If I called her, Carlton might have found out, and she'd get in trouble."

I'd messed around with a woman out of my league before. I knew the rules.

"So," Rembrandt said, "Tina sent you here?"

"Tina told me about your robbery warrant."

"If the cops are on their way…" He scrunched his face.

"She hasn't told them about you. Not yet at least."

"I should pack up and go."

"That's why I'm here. Hopefully, you can give me some info that we can work with and keep the cops away from you."

"That would be nice." Rembrandt nodded. "That would be real nice. All right. What do you want to know?"

"Were you two together yesterday morning?"

He nodded.

"What time did she show up?"

"Around five."

"That's mighty early for a hook-up."

Rembrandt shrugged. "We do what we have to. She sneaks away under the pretense of going to the gym. Sometimes the mall."

Pretense was an interesting word choice. He seemed to be a smart guy, but why the trouble with the law as a kid then the robbery warrant? Maybe he had a temper under the artsy exterior. Is that what drew Tina to him? Mike had a temper. Carlton had a temper.

"Sometimes," Rembrandt continued, "we got together when Carlton went out with his friends."

"You were a kept man."

"I'm not complaining."

"Is it because of the warrant?"

He shrugged. "I sort of stepped on myself with that."

"Tina said you broke into a gallery to take back one of your art pieces."

"That's a simplified version of the story, but yeah, basically."

"Then you assaulted the gallery's owner, which took it to a robbery charge."

Rembrandt's eyes narrowed. "You sound like a cop."

"Was one."

"I've got a lawyer—not a good one—but he's trying to resolve the issues through some backchannels."

"Greasing the skids?"

"If I had money, I wouldn't be in this predicament."

"What kind of back channels are you talking about?"

"Favors for favors."

I frowned. I didn't understand what he was intimating.

Rembrandt looked away for a moment. "Some doors open when people learn you have money issues and a certain proclivity toward art."

Proclivity was yet another interesting word selection. Maybe Tina liked the guy because he was unlike Carlton and Mike. I could imagine Rembrandt reading books and drinking coffee somewhere. That was something I couldn't envision the hotheaded Mike or uber-athletic Carlton ever doing. On the dresser, near the television, were several books.

"Those doors," Rembrandt said, "were not something I wanted to walk through. I may have no choice, though."

"Counterfeit art?"

"That's one avenue, but there are others, and they all pay. And if one of those roads keeps me out of prison, maybe it's worth traveling for a bit. Until then, I'm hiding here."

"What about Tina?"

"She knows. I didn't hide anything from her."

Thinking about the divorce papers that Butch Hollingshead mentioned, I asked, "Did she ever discuss divorcing Carlton?"

"Tina had no intention of doing that." He didn't sound disappointed.

"You never talked about it? No pillow talk about what things might be like if the two of you ever ran away together?"

"You have Tina confused with another woman."

Maybe I did.

"I'm not sure how much you know Tina, but that's not the type of woman she is. And that's not to say she isn't great because she is. If I had to say it, I might even love her, but she didn't love me back. I'm okay with it. That's the situation. Life isn't fair."

"Were you jealous of Carlton Winfrey?"

"Of course I was. But that didn't mean I wanted to kill the man."

"You wanted Tina to leave the relationship."

"I didn't say that."

"You said you might love her."

"So? Just like life, love isn't fair. And Tina is a woman accustomed to a certain life. It's a life I can't afford to give her."

"That's why she stayed with Carlton?"

"That's one reason."

"What's another?"

"She was afraid."

"Of getting hit?"

Rembrandt shrugged. "There was emotional stuff, too. Telling her she's fat and ugly and not worth keeping around. Do you know how hard she worked to keep that body? She's a freak when it comes to food and exercise. Too much. Again, not that I'm complaining."

"You've seen a lot in two months."

"Two? Who said that? We've been together for six."

Why had Tina downplayed the length of their relationship? If Rembrandt and Tina had been involved for two months or six didn't make any difference to me.

"If she was afraid of Carlton," I said, "why would she risk angering him further by cheating on him?"

Rembrandt crossed his legs in the chair and sat almost meditatively. His wrists rested on his knees, and his hands dangled down. "That's a good question. I never really thought about it. I mean, she's hot, right? And I was kind of bowled over by her interest in me, but if I had to guess, she probably risked it for compassion. Carlton wasn't the most caring person. Maybe he was when they first got together, but not lately."

"Do you think Tina is capable of murdering Carlton?"

He pursed his lips, and his eyes drifted to the corner of the room. "This stays between you and me?"

I nodded. "If it has to."

"It does. I would never say this to the cops."

"Then it'll stay between us."

"In that case, yeah, I definitely think she could have killed him."

"But what about that whole bit about not wanting a divorce due to her comfortable lifestyle."

He lifted a hand. "Thinking her capable is a whole lot different than believing she did it."

I cocked my head.

"Do I think she did it? Not a chance but listen. Tina wasn't happy. Yeah, she stayed out of comfort and fear, but a woman will only take that kind of life for so long. Then something is going to break." He snapped his fingers. "When it does, what it'll look like is anyone's business."

"Sounds like you speak from experience."

"My father beat my mother. One day she turned around and brained him with a skillet—a real cast iron beast. She used to make fried chicken with it. I was at school when it happened, so I missed the whole thing. She went to jail for a while, and he raised me after he came home from the hospital. When she got out, things were different. Better. He never raised a hand to her again."

"Did you tell this story to Tina?"

"Sure, but I told her to hit Carlton with a frying pan, not stab him with a knife."

I stood. "Thank you for your time."

"Are you going to call the cops?"

"No. Tina wanted to protect you, and you've been helpful."

Rembrandt clasped his hands together as if in prayer. "I appreciate that."

"I'm not sure how long it will keep the cops away, though."

"Maybe I should pack and go."

"If you want to stay off the radar, it's probably a good idea."

I left without looking back.

***

Several Coeur d'Alene police cars raced into the parking lot as I walked out of the hotel. Their emergency lights were active, but their sirens were silent. I stopped to watch.

The vehicles stopped in front of the hotel, and officers bailed out. They hurried by me. Equipment noisily jangled from their hips. Once they were inside, I continued walking.

At the truck, Mike grinned widely.

"What did you do?" I asked.

"What do you think?"

I didn't get into the truck and stalked toward the lake. Mike caught up near the beach.

"What's wrong?" he said.

"You're an asshole."

"You already told me that."

"I'm telling you again."

He pointed at the hotel. "But that guy had a warrant."

"What if he did? He confirmed Tina's alibi."

"Great! Let him tell the cops so she can walk away from

this crap.”

I tapped my temple. “Stop thinking like a cop.”

“I *am* a cop.”

“You’re working for the defense now, moron.”

Mike pulled his shoulders back and set his jaw. “I did what was right.”

“No, you didn’t. You did what fed your ego.”

I turned to leave, but Mike grabbed me.

“That son of a bitch deserved to get grabbed.”

“You still don’t get it.”

“What don’t I get?”

I lifted my hands in frustration. “Tina’s in jail.”

“I *know*.”

“Accused of murder.”

“I know.”

I smirked. “That’s great you realize it because you handed the cops another motive for murdering her husband—an illicit love affair.”

Mike looked away.

“I promised Tina that we wouldn’t call the cops, and you made me a liar.”

“I did it to help,” he said.

“You did it because you were jealous. News flash, pal. She left you.” I tapped his chest, and he smacked my hand away. “She doesn’t love you, and she doesn’t want you back.”

His lips tightened, and tears welled in his eyes.

“Tina moved on,” I said. “You should, too.”

I brushed by him, banging into his shoulder, and headed toward my truck. Mike didn’t follow.

Chapter 11

Erika arrived a little before eleven.

I heard her car pull up outside moments before a key slid into the front door. She didn't call out. Maybe she thought I was sleeping.

She took her time entering the room. When she did, she was naked, backlit by the television running the evening news. Wordlessly, Erika climbed onto the bed and kissed me.

Thoughts raced through my mind.

Should I apologize for how dinner went the previous evening?

Did she forgive me?

Was she going to ask me to stop helping Tina?

I stopped worrying and fell deeper into her kiss.

***

Afterward, we went to the kitchen for some toast. Neither of us was a culinary expert, nor were we choosy in moments like this. Erika sprinkled some cinnamon and sugar on hers. I put too much butter on mine.

Corporal lay in the corner and panted.

Erika wore one of my *Security* t-shirts from the club. I had on a pair of shorts. The house was stuffy, and toasting bread seemed to add to the late June heat.

"You need an air conditioner," she said.

"I rent. Remember?"

She nibbled on her toast. "Maybe you can get one of

those window units. Couple hundred bucks. We wouldn't sweat so much."

"I like when you sweat. You taste salty."

Erika studied her toast. She didn't look up when she asked, "How's Mike?"

"Fine."

Now, her eyes challenged mine. "You know. You just don't want to say."

I carefully set my toast down. "He's not the same."

"What if he is?"

"We already went over this."

She bit into her toast again. After swallowing, she said, "A year ago, I ran into a friend from high school—Carrie."

The name didn't sound familiar, and my brow furrowed as I ran through the mental Rolodex of Erika's friends.

"You haven't met her. If you're lucky, you won't." She picked at the corner of her toast. "Back in school, we used to go to all the parties. Drank some beer. Smoked some weed."

I cocked my head.

"Yes, Officer Cutler. I smoked weed, and, no, I don't do that anymore."

"I don't care if you do."

"That's not the point. We did a little back then, but not much. I never thought it was that great. Carrie said the same thing. Mostly we smoked it so we could fit into the cool circles. Same thing with the beer."

"Peer pressure."

She shook her head. "No one pressured us to do any of it. We just did it. All of it was our choice. We thought it would make us cool." She smiled wryly. "Well, cooler. So anyway, I ran into Carrie at Dick's, and she looked like hell. She was twitching like crazy, and her face has all those blisters on them."

"Meth mites."

"Which is sad, you know, because she used to be pretty. Blond and a nice figure. About my height. The boys loved her. Not now. She looked like one of the bar towels at the club—grayish, wrung-out, ready for the trash. Smelled as bad, too."

I crinkled my nose.

"Anyway, Carrie asked if I could buy her a burger, and I agreed. We sat and talked for a while. I asked what she'd been doing since high school, and she said, 'a little of this and a little of that' and then told me all the jobs she'd had over the years. Really laid it on like she was a big success, but the way she looked, she hadn't done anything unless it was illegal."

As a cop, I'd seen the junkie con many times—the complete overselling of bullshit. Often it worked because the mark relents. Maybe the mark had compassion for the junkie's plight. Or the mark simply acquiesced so the junkie would go away. Either way, the junkie viewed the result as a successful manipulation of their skills. Junkies lie to themselves better than anyone else.

Erika continued. "I asked her about her drug use. At first, she downplayed it. Said they had been a fun part of her life, but it was time she grew up. Move on and get in with society, so to speak. Then she asked if she could borrow twenty bucks. She needed to get some medicine."

I didn't ask if she gave the money to Carrie. I didn't want to know.

"But here's the thing. We were the same up until high school ended. Hell, maybe even after it ended. She went to one semester of college then dropped out. Just like me. So, what's different?"

"A lot of things could be different," I said. "Maybe it was her upbringing. Maybe something happened in her life you don't know about. Maybe she found new friends, and they led her down that path."

Erika shrugged. "And maybe she was always that way. Back in school, she was the one who took us to the parties. She knew who to scam weed from. She tried shrooms once. I was too afraid to do it, but not her. If she was willing to do that stuff in school, maybe it got worse later."

I saw where she was leading this conversation. "And you think Mike has always had racist tendencies?"

She stared at me.

"What if he has? It doesn't change the fact that there's a woman accused of a murder I don't think she committed."

"And you want to keep helping her?"

"As long as I'm getting paid for it, why not?"

That gave her pause. I told her about Butch Hollingshead and his offer. I also told her about Rembrandt Easton and the lies Tina told surrounding him.

"And your friend saw this Rembrandt?"

"He did."

"And how did he react?"

"About as you'd expect. He hit the man."

"So, he's twisted up."

"To say the least."

Erika asked, "What else is going on?"

I cocked my head.

"The tone of your voice. There's something you're not saying."

"It's you," I said.

"Me?"

"You're the woman I—" Erika leaned in slightly, and I

almost said the words right there, but the timing seemed all wrong. "I want to be with."

"And her?"

"She's not like I remember."

"Like Mike?"

"More like your friend, Carrie."

Erika bit into her toast. She tossed the remaining bread toward Corporal, who devoured it in a single bite. "Keep helping her, but don't forget how I feel in this."

"I won't."

Chapter 12

In the morning, I showered and quietly left the house. Erika remained in bed. She planned to get as much sleep as possible. Working the club that weekend promised to be a long and exhausting experience.

As I passed through downtown, the physical signs of a basketball tournament were present. Portable hoops lined the sidewalks. When the business world shut down after five, the city would close the streets, and workers would wheel the nets into their rightful places. Hoopfest, the world's largest three-on-three street basketball tournament, was set to begin first thing tomorrow morning.

In Coeur d'Alene, I met Butch Hollingshead at his Sherman Avenue office. He'd left a voicemail last night asking me to stop by in the morning. His receptionist, an attractive woman with a librarian's demeanor, handed me a clipboard of paperwork to fill out. At least, I would get paid for my time now. When I finished, she escorted me to his office.

Butch waved me in and pointed to one of the red leather chairs in front of his desk.

He closed a blue folder and picked up a yellow notepad. "Tina's upset."

"Duh."

Butch cocked his head.

"She's in jail."

"She's not upset about that. Well, that's not what I meant. She's upset over some guy named," he consulted the notepad, "Rembrandt—"

"Easton," I interrupted.

The notepad slid from Butch's fingers. "You know the guy?"

I nodded.

He interlaced his fingers and tapped his thumbs together while studying me. Butch wore a slightly wrinkled white shirt and a red tie that was loosened around the neck. Although it was barely nine, he looked as if he'd been at the office for hours.

I asked, "How did she find out about Rembrandt's arrest?"

"I mentioned it to her."

"And how did you learn about it?"

With a thud, Butch dropped his hands to the desk. "One of the prosecuting attorneys gave me a heads up."

"Isn't that bordering on unethical behavior?"

His brow furrowed. "They're supposed to share what they have."

"But Easton was arrested on an unrelated out-of-state warrant."

"So?"

"The prosecutor wouldn't have to tell you about him. Not until they linked him with Tina's case."

The attorney's face relaxed. "Let's just say we tend to play a gentlemanly game of liar's poker before discovery. The truth would eventually come out during pre-trial, but my friend and I tend to send the other on wild goose chases. I'm sure he was testing to see how good of a lead this Rembrandt Easton was. He casually mentioned the man's name when we were talking about another case. It was so informal that I knew Mr. Easton must have been important somehow." Butch smoothed his tie. "Now, being the exceptional liar that I am, I simply stared at my friend and refused to nibble the bait. But did I want to? Maybe. Had I asked, my friend would have sunk the hook deep and reeled me in."

Lawyers, I thought. Even the games they play are shifty.

"I couldn't understand the importance of Mr. Easton then, so I checked him out. That's when I discovered the Los Angeles warrant and his recent local arrest. At that point, I had an inkling of his significance. There's an old saying about measuring twice and cutting once."

"You don't look like a carpenter," I said.

"My father taught it to me. The same thing goes for evidence. Trust but verify. I dug deeper into that local arrest and asked a friend in the records department to pull the CAD report on how Mr. Easton was found."

"You have a lot of friends on the other side of the fence."

He spread his hands wide. "It's a small town."

"And you're a friendly guy."

"Thank you for noticing. Do you know how Mr. Easton was found? Of course, you do."

I stared at him. What was there to say?

"But that still didn't answer the question of Mr. Easton's relevance to Tina Winfrey's case. So, I asked if she knew him." He pantomimed an exploding head.

"I would imagine."

"After that, we had a long conversation about being truthful with her lawyer. It's not a good sign when your client holds things back."

"We had a similar conversation."

"You did?" He leaned forward. "And she told you she didn't want Mr. Easton involved."

I shrugged.

"For what it's worth, I'm glad he's in custody. I would have preferred it be handled a different way. Maybe have him surrender through me. Regardless, this kind of stuff comes out one way or the other. But I'd rather it come out now than later. I hate surprises, and an extramarital boyfriend is more than problematic. We can address it here and now, maybe figure a way to minimize the damage, and be ready when this thing goes to trial—*if* it goes to trial."

"If?"

"It's still early. Have you found anything that can help?"

"We found Easton."

He smirked. "Speaking of we, where is your sidekick?"

"I don't know."

"I'm sensing some problems."

"We're fine," I lied.

"In that case, when you talk with him, let him know the homicide detectives want to re-interview him."

"They called you?"

"No. My friend—the prosecuting attorney—he mentioned it. They want to follow up on Mike's story. I'm sure they want to see if he'll recant and change it—maybe catch him in a lie, too."

"And what did you say?"

"I said I'd help." He smiled. "As I said, I'm an exceptional liar. When you talk with him, reiterate the importance of not changing his story. If what he said was the truth, then he should stick with it."

"Nobody lies but you."

His smile faded. "There is an appropriate time and place for a lie. And it can never jam a client or me up. Now, Mike doesn't have to run down and talk with the detectives, but sooner or later, he's going to have to."

"Anything else?"

"I'd like you to interview Olivia Wagner, the witness who saw Tina's car the morning Carlton was murdered. Supposedly, she saw it in the driveway at five in the morning." Butch flipped open the folder and turned a couple of pages. He jotted an address on a yellow sticky note then handed it to me. "Find out what she was doing up at that hour."

"Is that all she gave them?"

He flipped through the file to reveal a short police report. "The woman said she saw Tina's car that morning. That was it. By itself, it's not that damaging" He tossed the file onto the desk. "This should have been a slam dunk. If Tina had told the truth about her boyfriend, she would have had an alibi. Instead, she lied. The second lie made her look even more guilty. I'm hoping the physical evidence will eventually clear her, but if there's any bias in the investigation, we're going to have a tough road."

"But her car being in the driveway at that hour is a problem."

"There are plenty of plausible scenarios for such a thing, but all are out the window now."

I tucked the sticky note into my pocket.

"The bail hearing is set for Monday, but it's only a dog and pony show now. The judge won't grant it."

"Why not?"

"She's a flight risk with access to money. This is one time being wealthy doesn't work in favor of the rich."

"Said the high-priced defense attorney." I stood. "I'll be in touch."

***

Olivia Wagner lived three doors away from Carlton Winfrey. The multi-level home was painted white with reddish-brown trim. A large porch with pillars graced the front. In the driveway sat a Volvo and a Toyota.

Before ascending the porch stairs, I turned around. The cul-de-sac setting would have allowed Olivia Wagner to look directly out her front window and see the Winfrey home's driveway. It seemed entirely plausible she could have seen Tina's vehicle that morning.

The late-June sun baked down, and the newspaper predicted the daily high would break the nineties. A bead of sweat rolled from under an armpit. It wasn't even noon.

After knocking, I stepped back and waited.

The door opened, and a woman in her sixties appeared. Her face carried a look of permanent surprise—the skin pulled taut from recent plastic surgery. She wore a yellow blouse that opened surprisingly low for a woman of her age—it revealed freckled cleavage. A pair of black slacks complemented a thin waist and long legs.

A blast of cool air escaped the house.

"Olivia Wagner?" I asked.

Her smile was polite, maybe even flattered, but it was hard to read with how tight her face was. "I'm Kay. Olivia is my daughter."

"John Cutler."

We shook hands. Hers was cool to the touch.

I continued. "I'm a private investigator hired by Mrs. Winfrey's attorney."

"A tragedy." Her gaze flicked over my shoulder. I presumed it was to the Winfrey home.

"Is Olivia in?"

Her eyes returned to me. "Yes."

"May I speak with her?"

"Do you have identification?"

I showed her both my driver's license and private investigator's license.

"You're from Washington."

"Right across the border."

"And you can work in Idaho?"

"According to Mrs. Winfrey's attorney, I can."

That seemed to appease her, and she motioned me in. It was probably ten degrees cooler inside the house. Maybe Erika was right—I should consider an air-conditioning unit.

Kay directed me into the living room. A large couch and two oversized chairs sucked up most of the space. Their fabric complimented an Oriental rug that rested over the dark, hardwood floor. A grandfather clock stood guard over it all.

Japanese-inspired art was everywhere. On a far wall hung a black and white painting of a lone samurai kneeling next to a fallen comrade. The warrior seemed to be crying and, at the exact moment, proud of the dead man. A scroll with Japanese characters was displayed nearby.

Kay noticed my interest. "Do you like nihonga?"

"I'm sorry?"

"These Japanese paintings."

"They're nice. I've never paid much attention to the form before." I pointed to the scroll. "What's this mean?"

"It's Zen. It means the obstacle is the path."

I had no idea what that meant.

Her lips formed into another tight smile. The skin around her eyes didn't crinkle when she did, though. It made for an unsettling display of happiness.

"My husband," Kay said as she moved toward the samurai picture, "was very much into their culture. He was there in the sixties while in the service and fell in love with their history and how they lived." Her smile vanished. "I think he might have fallen for a girl there. Dale never said." It was an odd admission from a woman I'd just met. "We were supposed to visit there again this year. It had been some time since our last trip."

Kay's eyes seemed unfocused now, and they misted over.

I stood uncomfortably still in the room and watched the woman. I wanted to cough and interrupt her private thoughts, but it was clear she struggled with something. So, I froze like a quiet spectator and waited.

Her eyes soon refocused, and she faced me. "I apologize. Even after a year, it still gets me."

"It's okay."

She touched the picture's frame. "You're not here to watch a woman mourn." Kay then directed me toward one of the oversized chairs. "Wait here while I fetch Olivia. But I must warn you, she hasn't quite recovered from her father's death either. With the anniversary of his passing, she's been plagued with a bout of melancholy."

When Kay drifted away, I scanned the photographs in the room. On the table next to me was a framed picture of a gray-haired man in Bushido gear. A broad smile creased his face, and his blue eyes shone brightly.

On the low, dark wood coffee table was another photo of the same man. He reclined on a boat with Kay under one arm and a young, blond girl under the other. His tanned skin and perfectly white teeth showed the pride he took in his appearance.

Dale Wagner may have died last year, but he lived on through his family. His unexpected death had taken its toll. The living remorse weighed heavily on the house.

Kay returned several minutes later with a woman who walked timidly behind her. She was an older version of the young, blond girl in the photo.

I stood and stepped around the coffee table.

Olivia Wagner's hands were clasped tightly in front of her. She appeared to be in her mid-thirties. Her blue jeans and t-shirt hung from her body and gave the impression that she had experienced some recent weight loss but hadn't bothered to change her wardrobe. Her face was freshly washed and free of any make-up. She had her father's eyes.

I considered offering my hand, but Olivia's body language felt off—as if she were afraid of my presence.

She sat in the chair across from the couch, but her eyes never left me—a scared girl lurked behind them. Kay lingered in the corner of the room.

After sitting on the couch, I said, "Olivia, I'm John Cutler. Mrs. Winfrey's attorney has hired me."

"My mother told me."

"I'd like to ask about what you saw the other morning."

"I've already talked to the police."

I nodded. "Yes, ma'am. This is only to verify what they wrote in their report." I made my words and tone as gentle as possible. If she was still dealing with her father's death after a year, what kind of relationship did they have? Was she his little princess and the world without him was too hard to bear? "Mrs. Winfrey has been arrested for the murder of her husband. We're attempting to build her defense."

Olivia brought her feet onto the chair and crossed her arms around her legs, pulling them in tight to her—an extra barrier for me to get through. "I understand," she muttered.

"According to the police report, you saw Tina's car

parked in the driveway the morning Carlton Winfrey was murdered."

Her left hand gripped the fingers of her right. "That's correct."

"What kind of car does Tina drive?"

"A Jaguar. A red one. She's driven it since they moved in. And before you ask, yes, I'm certain it was her car."

The way she answered it made it seem like she wasn't happy that they were neighbors.

"How long have the Winfrey's lived here?"

"Just this year. I think they're renting."

More disdain in her voice. Was it the fact that they were renters in the neighborhood, or was it something else? Was I on edge for racism because of the recent run-in with Mike? I tried to push the thoughts away and focus on the facts.

"Were there problems with the Winfreys as your neighbors?"

"No."

I glanced to Kay, who shook her head. Returning my gaze to Olivia, I asked, "And you're sure you saw Tina's car that morning?"

"Yes," she said, setting her jaw. "I'm positive the car was there, and I'm positive it was hers." Her tone was forceful.

"She denies she was there."

"She's lying."

There was no fear or disdain in that statement. Of everything she had said so far, this was the one she hadn't hesitated on.

"Have you ever met Tina?"

Olivia shook her head.

"What about her husband?"

"No."

From the corner, Kay cocked her head and watched her daughter with interest. When she noticed me, Kay straightened and looked away.

I leaned forward to better study Olivia Wagner. "You've never met Carlton Winfrey?"

She averted her eyes. "Not really."

"That's different than no."

Olivia shrugged. "His friends invited me to a couple of parties."

"Did you go?"

"No. Definitely not." Her brow furrowed, and the way she looked at me was intended to make me feel stupid.

"Why didn't you go?"

"My fiancé wouldn't approve."

"He wouldn't have gone to the party?"

She averted her eyes.

Okay, now I knew I was looking for hints of racism, and it felt like I found them. Could Olivia have reported seeing Tina's car in the driveway simply to have gotten her in trouble? Or could her fiancé have suggested she do such a thing?

"Who's your fiancé?"

"Do you really need his name?"

"I figure it's better to ask my questions at one time and not have to come back and bother you later."

She hesitated and glanced back at her mother.

"Tell him, honey," Kay said.

Olivia inhaled deeply, then said, "Scott Fairchild."

"And where does Scott live?"

Once more, Olivia looked toward her mother. Kay motioned to me.

The younger Wagner sighed, then recited her fiancé's

address. I jotted it in my notebook. When I was done, I looked up. "Where do you work, Olivia?"

"I don't." She seemed embarrassed at the revelation. "Not now, at least."

"But you did?"

"Before my father died. I've been out of sorts since—"

"Do you work out?"

Irritation replaced her embarrassment. "What are you asking?"

"I'm trying to understand what you were doing up so early that morning."

Her feet dropped to the floor, and she leaned forward. Her hands gripped the seat cushions. "My father died a year ago. Maybe that wouldn't bother you, but it has me. I don't sleep particularly well anymore. I went outside to smoke a cigarette on Tuesday morning. My mother doesn't approve."

Kay turned away at the comment.

I said, "My mother never approved of my smoking either."

That seemed to lighten her mood. A corner of her lip rose in a sardonic smile.

"And you're sure of the time?" I asked.

"One hundred percent. I checked before I went outside." She motioned toward the grandfather clock.

"Did you see anything else?"

Olivia shook her head.

"Can you tell me anything else about Mr. and Mrs. Winfrey?"

"We didn't interact."

I lowered my head and thought. What else could I ask her? The only thing she had told the police was about seeing Tina's car in the driveway. According to Butch

Hollingshead, she didn't provide anything more damaging than that.

But how was the car in the driveway if Tina was spending time with Rembrandt at the resort? Of everything, Olivia's adamant statement about Tina's lying stuck with me. She'd already been caught lying to the police. Was she lying about not murdering her husband?

There was nothing further to ask. I stood and tucked my notebook away. This time, I did offer my hand. Olivia hesitantly took it. Her palm was warm.

She stayed seated while Kay escorted me out of the house.

"I apologize if my visit caused any problems this morning."

"It's all right, Mr. Cutler." Kay patted my arm. "She's still adjusting to the loss of her father."

Chapter 13

Erika arrived at my house an hour before our scheduled shift at the club. She wore denim shorts and tennis shoes while I had on jeans and black boots. Her clothes were for comfort and earning tips while mine were fighting. We both had on black t-shirts emblazoned with the Club Royale logo. Her shirt was form-fitting and looked tremendous. Mine had a bright yellow Security scrawled across the back.

"You look great," I said.

She shrugged. "Same thing I wear every day."

"Still."

"Where's the dog?"

"Out back. Watered and set for the night."

Erika dropped into my desk chair and absently thumbed through the papers on the desk.

"You ready to go?" I asked.

Another shrug. This one was less enthusiastic than the last.

"Everything okay?"

"It's this weekend," she said. "If I could skip it, I would."

I understood. Of any event weekend to work at the bar, Hoopfest was the worst.

According to the newspaper, the three-on-three basketball tournament was the largest in the world. Over six thousand teams made up of four people each were expected to swarm the downtown streets for the next two days. With friends and family in attendance, the event would attract over 250,000 people. The elimination tournament would start on Saturday morning and culminate with the championship game on Riverfront Park's center court late Sunday afternoon.

The whole weekend was big business. City-approved vendors set up booths or wandered through the tournament hawking wares. Again, the newspaper estimated that the tourney pumped almost $40 million into the local economy. Of course, that's the happy, promotional stuff that brings in the tourists. It's the dirty side of the tournament that rarely gets talked about.

"It'll be okay," I said.

She eyed me. "It's not your ass getting grabbed."

I feigned offense. "My ass gets grabbed plenty."

"It better not."

"Sometimes."

"Is that a fact?" She leaned back in the chair. "You don't seem too concerned about this weekend."

"What's there to be worried about?" I tried to sound untroubled. I had bounced the previous two Hoopfest weekends. The idea of another tourney weekend filled me with dread I never felt as a cop.

Throughout the tournament, fights occurred. Players hopped up on a cocktail of adrenaline and summer heat had little self-control when tempers flared. Many players flocked to the competition to claim some long-forgotten courtside glory.

During the day, the police department flooded the streets with its officers. It was an attempt to convince the public that it was safe. Peace through superior firepower.

Friday night was generally peaceful, but Saturday night was volatile. All bars filled regardless of their local popularity. Most nightclubs packed to overcapacity.

Drunk bodies banged into other drunk bodies. That's when the emotional highs of competition slammed into the misery of early tournament eliminations. Dangerous things happened then.

Suspected gang members seemed to be attracted to the event. Maybe they played in the tournament. Perhaps they came to conduct illicit business. Or perhaps they only wanted to be around for a good time. Whatever it was, the city and its tourist bureau turned a blind eye to their arrival. It was best not to call too much attention to the problem of visiting hooligans.

A predominantly white city frowning upon the arrival of any minority segment might be viewed as racist. Also, just mentioning a possible uptick in criminal activity could hurt the event's participation numbers. It would be a lose-lose for city hall, so it was no wonder why they remained silent.

However, the cops must have been aware of it. The presence of so many uniformed officers and plain-clothes liquor control board agents proved it.

Three years in a row, Spokane had experienced a nighttime shooting related to the bar scene. The year before I arrived, a mini-riot occurred that sent several gunshot victims to the hospital.

"Ready to go?" I asked.

"As ready as I'll ever be." She stood. "Your car or mine?"

Due to the limited parking and the fact we would both come back here, we decided last week to travel together.

"Your car," I said. "It's smaller."

I expected her to bring it up, but she waited until we passed the Maxwell House and turned southbound on Ash Street before she did.

"Did you work on your friend's problem today?"

"I did."

She glanced at me. There was no hostility in her face. "Well? Tell me."

"I interviewed a witness who said she saw Tina's car the morning of the murder."

"And that proves what? That the wife murdered her husband?"

"Not really, but it proved Tina lied about her whereabouts."

"What was she doing?"

"Spending time with her boyfriend."

Erika frowned. "She's married."

"I know."

"I thought you said she was nice."

"She is. *Was*." I shook my head. "I don't know anymore, but there's a huge difference between an extramarital affair and murder."

"So, the witness—what about her?"

"I don't know. Something was off there."

Erika changed lanes. "What was wrong with her?"

"Tough to say. Her father died last year, and her mom says she's still broken up about it. The woman barely reacted to my being there. I got the feeling that I could have vanished into a puff of smoke, and she wouldn't have blinked twice."

"But she was credible?"

"Seemed so. I mean, her mom seemed normal, and it's a nice neighborhood—"

"Where a murder occurred," Erika interrupted.

"There's that."

"Could she have been on drugs or something? Prescription meds, maybe?"

"I didn't get that vibe."

"What did Mike think?"

"He wasn't there."

"Where was he?"

"No idea."

Ash Street merged with Maple, and we crossed the bridge over the Spokane River. I stared off into the valley below.

Erika asked, "How did you find out about the witness?"

"Tina's attorney."

"So, this is a paying job."

"It is."

"Where was Mike?"

"I don't know. I haven't heard from him since our argument yesterday."

"Are you worried?"

"Mike's a grown man."

"Do you think he's doing something stupid?"

"Probably."

I didn't tell her that I had stopped at Mike's hotel after the interview with Olivia Wagner, but he wasn't there. I had also called to update Butch Hollingshead, and he informed me that Mike hadn't checked in.

"This isn't his home," I said, "so he doesn't have friends or contacts. He shouldn't just fall off the radar. But if there's one thing I know, he's not leaving. Tina's still in jail. That alone means he's around."

Erika turned on First Avenue. "What's the next step?"

"I'd like to talk with Carlton's friends. Maybe they'll tell me something they haven't shared with the cops."

"Do you think they'll talk with you?"

I shrugged. "Won't know until I try. I might also track down Olivia Wagner's fiancé."

"Who?"

"The witness who saw Tina's car."

"Oh. Why do you want to interview her fiancé?"

"A feeling, I guess. Sometimes just going through the motion helps. It'll probably be a waste of gas and time."

"Ugh," Erika grunted as we stopped at the Post Street intersection.

Our path ahead was blocked off. Portable basketball hoops now stood like sentries in the middle of the streets. The guardians of the asphalt nullified all vehicular traffic.

She glanced over her shoulder, signaled, and turned south onto Post. "I forget how screwed up the streets get for this stupid event."

"That's not civic-minded."

"Bite me."

"With pleasure."

She smirked as the car accelerated toward Third Avenue. "So, when are you going to do all this detecting?"

"Tomorrow."

"After a long night at the club?"

"It's got to be done."

"Okay, fine. I'll go with." She noticed me watching her. "Consider it couple time."

"Oh, that's what it'll be?"

"Unless you want to pay me, then you can consider me an employee, but either way, I'm going."

"Couple time, it is."

"I knew you'd see it my way."

"I usually do."

She laughed. "Oh, my God, I wish."

I stopped talking then. I knew better than to continue and dig myself further into that hole.

Chapter 14

Later the next morning, Erika and I drove to Coeur d'Alene. We silently ate Egg McMuffins and sipped coffees while we traveled. We weren't annoyed with each other; we were simply tired. I suggested that she stay in bed and get some extra sleep, but Erika stubbornly insisted she go with me.

The night at the club had been relatively quiet. No fights occurred inside the building, and only a couple of skirmishes erupted outside in the quiet streets now guarded by the basketball hoop sentries.

As bouncers, we never broke up an outside fight if it wasn't on our sidewalk. Technically, the liquor control board considered the sidewalk part of the establishment, and they'd annotate in the official file that a fight occurred there. But they also figured that an altercation in the street was beyond our control. So, if we could push the brawlers into the road, we'd claim the skirmish started there. All we needed was plausible deniability to keep the club's record clean. Let the cops deal with it. They're the ones with the fantastic health care plans—not us.

I hated bouncers when I was a cop. Now, I understand exactly why they acted that way.

Our first stop upon arriving in Coeur d'Alene was Mike's hotel. Erika went inside since I was unsuccessful yesterday. A few minutes later, she returned with a self-satisfied smirk. "He's still registered, but no one's seen him for a couple days."

"They told you that?"

"Yeah."

I pointed to the front of the hotel. "Yesterday, they said they couldn't share that information."

"It's probably how you asked."

"I asked nicely."

Erika ran the back of her hand down the length of her body. "Not as nice as I asked."

I dropped the truck into reverse. "Ain't that the truth."

***

After the motel, we stopped by the jail. Erika waited in the lobby while I talked with Tina.

Tina was sitting and waiting for me when I entered. As soon as I sat, she started.

"This place." She glanced back at the guard.

"What's going on?"

"They treat us like animals."

"It's not supposed to be a resort."

Her head snapped back to me. "You guys called the cops on Remmy."

I lifted my hands in mock surrender. "It wasn't supposed to happen."

"Why'd you do that?"

I paused, trying to think of a way to say it, but she read it on my face.

"Mike did it—didn't he?"

I shrugged.

She angrily slapped the counter, and everyone turned to look at her.

"Inmate," the guard said, "keep it in check, or you'll go back inside."

Tina lifted her hand but didn't turn around. It seemed

she was adjusting quickly to life behind bars.

"So, Mike hasn't been by?" I asked.

Her jaw flexed as her cheeks reddened. "He knows he's going to get a piece of my mind when he comes by."

"Probably."

Tina's face softened, and she cocked her head. "You haven't talked with him, either?"

"No."

"What happened?"

"I got pissed over the Rembrandt thing."

"You did?"

"I gave you my word, and he didn't respect that."

She looked down at her hands. "What about Butch? Has he heard from him?"

"No."

Tina rubbed her face. "Oh, Mike. You stupid bastard." She dropped her hands in resignation. "You know, I think he believes there's still a chance for us."

"He's banking on it."

She leaned forward and put her hands on the counter. "I can't make him understand that there's not. What do I have to do? Be cruel?"

"I don't know."

"There's no way we're getting back together."

"Then why call him?"

Tina flopped back into her chair. "Why can't he and I communicate like human beings? Like what we're doing?" She ruefully shook her head. "Even when I was doing it— talking with him— I knew somewhere in the back of my mind that it was a bad idea."

"It gave him hope."

"He's my ex for a reason, John. I don't want to travel that road again."

I pointed to the bruising under her eye. "Then why not call the cops in LA?"

"You know."

I did. Comfort.

"When there's a cop in the family, even an ex-husband, it's easy to call for advice. He was the first person I thought to phone. Not because we used to be married, but because he had a badge. Was it smart? It's easy to say no now. But I never led him on. I swear. I swear to God. All I wanted was to talk to a cop without actually talking to a cop. Do you understand?"

"Sure. I get it. People ask me questions all the time, and I haven't been one for years."

She put her head on the edge of the counter.

"Inmate," the guard said, "sit up straight."

Tina righted herself, and several people in the visiting room watched us.

"Animals," she whispered. "Fucking animals."

It was time to change the subject. I said, "Carlton's friends."

"What about them?"

"I need to interview them."

She grimaced. "They're not going to like you."

"I'm sure. How do I find them?"

"They always came to our house. I don't know where they live."

"Would they have headed back to LA?"

"Not likely."

I tilted my head. "Are they strapped for cash?"

"They're fine, I think, but they're supposed to play in Hoopfest. They'll stick around for that."

"After Carlton's murder?"

"Carlton wasn't on their team."

I tapped the counter. "The knee injury."

"There was that, but even if he wanted, he couldn't. The hazardous activities clause in his contract prevented it. And if his knee was healed, he would have been back with the team, and we would have been out of here."

"But he's dead less than a week."

"So?" Tina's face scrunched. "Stop thinking of them as Carlton's friends. Think of them like business associates, and you'll have a better picture. Have you watched that show Big Brother?"

"No."

"That's sort of how I see them. They're housemates, but they'll turn on each other to get an advantage."

"Doesn't sound like hometown friends."

"Like I said. Hey, I don't want those guys in my home. I told Butch that, and he was supposed to tell the cops."

"They've got a uniform stationed outside your house."

She nodded. "He told me. Not sure how much longer they're going to keep someone there. You can go in, look around if you need to. Your name should be on the list. Mike's, too. Do you think he's okay?"

"No."

"Because he's missing? Should you file a report or something?"

"Maybe you haven't noticed it because you've been too close or because he acts a different way around you, but Mike's..."

"What?"

"He's different."

Tina crossed her arms. "How so?"

"He's mean."

"Not to me."

"To the world in general."

"Because he's not over our divorce? I can't believe that."

I shrugged. "Believe it. He's convinced you're the one."

Her brow furrowed.

"The great love of his life that he's doing everything he can to get back."

She rolled her eyes.

"You don't believe in love?"

"Oh, I believe it," Tina said, "but it's transitory—always on the move."

"I understood transitory."

She leaned forward. "People come into our lives, and then they go. We share that time and hope to grow together. Sometimes that growth leads us in different directions, and we drift away. It's natural. We shouldn't fight it."

I considered the bruising under her eye again. She didn't seem able to drift away from Carlton Winfrey.

Tina continued. "We all float in some darkness. It's either spiritual or emotional, but it's darkness we must deal with. And no matter how temporary, we hope to find someone to act as a lighthouse to guide us to safety, to warmth, to love."

Her eyes darted briefly away. When they returned, she resumed in a manner as if she had practiced this monologue before.

"Some people get lucky and find that one person who will brighten their life forever. Their path is clear. Then some never find a lighthouse. They drift in the darkness until they finally drown in loneliness."

Was this the story she told herself on those nights when she and Winfrey fought? Was this the noble lie she clung to in the face of her pedestrian claims of comfort?

Tina tapped the counter. "And for some of us, we find several beacons along our journey—all of them burning bright and beckoning us to love's shore. But they aren't lighthouses we see, and soon we crash upon the rocks of despair." She had practiced this monologue before—I was sure of it. The rhythm and the words sounded like a preacher. "But we don't give in to hopelessness. We push off and drift back into the darkness, hoping to find another lighthouse."

I stared at her.

"That's who I am. That's who I remember you being, John."

"I need to go." I started to stand.

Tina reached out to stop me, but her hand stopped before passing over our cubicle's dividing wall.

When I sat again, she said, "I've had a lot of time to think in here."

I didn't believe that the lighthouse metaphor was a new idea. It sounded like it was something she'd considered and practiced for years. Did she think of it when she was married to Mike?

When I didn't say anything, she asked, "Are you in love, John?"

It wasn't a topic I wanted to discuss with her. "That's not relevant to what you and I are doing."

"No, it's not, but I'd still like to know."

We stared at each other for a few moments until I said, "Maybe. I think so."

"Then you're not."

I didn't like the finality of her statement.

"You're a searcher, John. It's in your eyes. It's always been. I could see it when you came for dinner way back when. You've never been happy with who you are."

That last statement cut too deep, and I stood abruptly. Tina reached over the dividing wall.

"Inmate!" the guard called and stepped forward.

She glanced back and apologetically waved. When she faced me again, she hurriedly said, "Listen, I'm sorry. I hope you are in love. Really."

But as I walked toward the door, I was filled with a sense of uncertainty.

Chapter 15

Erika and I were back on the freeway, headed to Spokane. Our next stop would be Hoopfest in hopes of finding Carlton's crew.

"What are their names?" she asked.

I dug out my notebook from my back pocket and flipped it open to the page from my first visit with Tina. I held it up so I could read and drive simultaneously. "JayJay Robinson, LaShaun Tate, Oscar Greene, and Andre Murphy."

"I thought you said they were in a gang—the Dead Boys or something."

"I did."

"The Dead Boys sounds like a rock band—one of those heavy metal groups—not a gang."

"They've got monikers."

Her face scrunched. "What the hell is a moniker?"

"A nickname."

"Then say nickname. It's got fewer syllables."

It took me a moment to quietly compare the two words by speaking them phonetically in my head. Okay, so she had a point about the syllables, but before I could comment, she continued.

"It's probably a cop thing." She lowered her voice to sound like a man. "The suspect had a moniker." Her head bounced side-to-side, and she continued to speak in that same low voice. "Moniker, moniker, moniker." Erika made sure to over-annunciate each syllable.

"Are you done?"

"Yeah."

"Still want to hear their nicknames?"

Erika barely hid her smirk. "Please."

"They call JayJay, Bumps."

"Weird."

"LaShaun answers to Bone."

She waggled her hand. "Okay, that's not so bad."

"Oscar is the Grouch."

"Sesame Street probably doesn't appreciate that."

"And Andre is known as Squirrel."

Erika faced me. "Squirrel?"

"That's what Tina said."

"Wow. They could all be Muppets."

I put my notebook on the console between us. "I don't know how they come up with the names."

"What court are they on?"

"I don't know."

"Then what's their team name?"

I eyed her.

"You didn't ask the name of the team?"

"I've never been to Hoopfest. I didn't know the teams had names."

She clucked her tongue loud enough to be heard over the engine. "There's got to be over a hundred thousand people downtown."

"The newspaper said a quarter of a million."

"How do you expect to find them without a team name?"

I shrugged. "Have some faith."

***

It was almost noon when we found a spot near

Riverside and Brown. We waited as a family with four kids loaded into their dented SUV—the vehicle left behind a plume of dark smoke as it headed away.

Downtown was completely blocked off, and parking was only available at the furthest edges of the city. We were three blocks from the first basketball courts and lucky to find a spot big enough for my truck. We should have brought Erika's car.

The noise from the tournament reached us as soon as we got out. People hurried by us on their way toward the action. Others wandered wearily back from it.

I held Erika's hand as we walked. "Let's find the information tent."

"What if we can't find them there?"

"Then we'll walk in the sun and spend the afternoon together."

"You're suddenly Mr. Romantic."

"There are worse ways to spend a day."

A couple of sunburnt teenagers ran by—each with a basketball under an arm. One of them bumped into Erika, and she fell into me.

After I righted her, she said, "I can think of better ways to spend our day."

Four twenty-somethings approached us. They were a blend of races—a poster team for the event. Each skin tone seemed represented. As they passed us, the white guy in the group got brave and chirped at Erika.

"Hey, baby, where you been all my life?" He flailed his arms wide.

His buddies laughed as he continued.

"Ditch your daddy and come play with us."

We didn't turn around, and Erika squeezed my hand.

The pale guy hollered one more time. "You don't know

what you're missing!"

When the group was out of earshot, Erika said, "Thank you."

"For?"

"Not letting that get to you."

I smiled, but it did bother me. It wasn't the fact that I was six years older than her. At our age, that gap was socially acceptable. What got to me was them running as a pack. The big mouth got to act tough because he had his friends with him. It was intimidation through numbers, and I had to keep my mouth closed because of it. I felt like a pussy.

One-on-one, I would have told him to shut his mouth or politely punched his teeth in. Hell, even two-on-one, I might have done the same thing. But four-on-one was so lopsided that taking on those odds could only be done as a last resort.

A sea of people ebbed and flowed through downtown. People of all makes and sizes wandered through the streets.

Some wore colorful costumes to bring fun to the weekend and grab some attention. In the crowd was an Uncle Sam, a pair of Blues Brothers, and a tutu-wearing Spider-man. On one court was a team of Star Wars geeks. The three guys actively playing wore tank tops and shorts along with Stormtrooper helmets. On the sideline, the head geek wore a Darth Vader helmet and cape.

Erika tapped the shoulder of a fan wearing a Star Wars shirt. The woman had been anxiously watching the game with hands clasped. The woman faced us with an open and happy expression.

"What's the team's name?" Erika asked.

The woman turned back toward the court. "The Redecoration Society of Alderaan."

Erika and I looked at each other then shrugged. Hoopfest brought out all types.

We passed some courts where the players banged away on each other like a tryout for the National Basketball Association. They yelled and taunted the other team. Some hollered for imaginary fouls. It was the ugly side of competition.

Near the heart of the tournament stood a large tent with makeshift counters. Volunteers wore the official Hoopfest t-shirt and greeted visitors.

"Can I help you?" a woman asked. She wore a white visor, and spiky gray hair peeked out above it.

I stepped up to the folding table. "How do we find where a team is playing?"

She picked up a clipboard. "Which team?"

"We don't know. We only know the players."

The woman frowned and set down her clipboard. "Give me a player's name."

"Oscar Greene."

She walked to the middle of the tent to consult a large binder.

Erika leaned in and whispered. "You should have given her his moniker."

I glared at her.

She stiffened her back and deepened her voice. "Moniker," she said.

Several people nearby turned toward us.

"Shut it," I whispered.

"Moniker?" she said with a lilt.

When my eyes bulged, Erika laughed. I couldn't help but join in.

The woman returned to the clipboard in front of us. "Oscar Greene is on Balls Deep."

"Gross," Erika muttered.

The woman slid a finger down the clipboard. When she reached the end of the paper, she flipped it over and slid to the middle of the next page. "Bracket one-sixty-one." She dropped the clipboard on the counter and flipped through yet another binder. "They're playing against Four Twenty over near Post and Riverside. In front of the STA Plaza. Court seventy-three."

As we proceeded toward the Spokane Transit Authority Plaza, the crowd thickened. Most seemed uninterested in moving out of our way. They had better things to do—either watching a game in progress or getting somewhere of their own. Regardless, it felt as if we were salmon swimming upstream through a bloated mass of humanity.

By their weaving and swaying, a few of the watchers appeared intoxicated. Most of the downtown bars were open and seemed to be doing a brisk business.

When we found the bus plaza, we asked a tournament monitor for directions to court seventy-three. He pointed to the street corner.

Erika motioned toward the plaza, "I need to go inside."

"For?"

She made a silly face.

"Oh. Let me go see how far into the game they are, and I'll meet you."

Erika spun on her heel and hurried away.

At court seventy-three, a game was in progress. Three black men played against three skinny white males with long hair. The pale guys looked like a crew of stoners decided to sign up for a basketball tournament. They played the way they looked—sloppy.

Two men—one black male and the other white—waited to be substituted in from the sidelines.

The team of black men wore red basketball jerseys with their monikers—nicknames—monogrammed in white across their shoulders.

Oscar "Grouch" Greene was a big man with a low forehead and menacing eyes. He looked like he was in his late twenties. His moniker, an obvious tie to his first name, seemed to suit his disposition. The lanky stoner guarding him appeared helpless and noticeably upset by the banging and elbowing Oscar.

JayJay "Bumps" Robinson was a fat guy with shorts down to his knees and socks up to his calves. Only his knees remained uncovered. He gasped as he shuffled around the court. He clapped for the ball since he clearly couldn't call for it. The longhaired guy guarding him grinned as if he'd just won the lottery.

Andre "Squirrel" Murphy was a tall man with a loping run and an unkempt afro that bounced as he moved. His trash-talking never stopped, much to the dismay of the stoner guarding him.

The fourth team member was sitting on the curb across the street and intently watching the game. I couldn't read the name on the back of his jersey, but it wasn't hard to guess who he was— LaShaun "Bone" Tate—the alpha male.

"Hustle to the corner, Bumps!" Bone yelled.

JayJay Robinson raised a hand in acknowledgment.

Bone cupped his hands around his mouth. "To the top, Squirrel."

Andre Murphy dribbled the ball toward the half-court line.

"C'mon, Grouch. Shake that bitch."

Oscar Greene elbowed his man then moved toward the rim.

Murphy passed the ball to Greene, who shot an easy layup.

Bone smiled and clapped. "That's how you do it."

A gray-haired woman behind a folding table flipped over a red card, changing the score to 11-6.

I stepped forward to a young woman sitting on the curb. "What do they play to?"

She didn't divert her attention from the game. "Twenty."

There was plenty of time to head inside the bus plaza and find Erika. People milled about inside the air-conditioned building even though buses were redirected around downtown for the weekend. Most were doing what I was doing—finding a restroom—or getting out of the sun for a few moments.

The plaza was built sometime in the previous decade and full of underutilized space. A mini-mart, a pizza shop, and several permanently vacant suites were on the second floor. On non-event weekends, the building remained a magnet for the city's malcontents. It was quasi-governmental efficiency at its best.

A line of about twenty women waited outside the women's restroom. There was no such delay for the men's room. As I approached, Erika walked out.

"Did you miss me?" she asked.

"I did. Wait here for a minute."

I headed inside the men's room. A couple of moments later, I returned to find Erika standing with her arms crossed. Irritation registered on her face.

"It's not fair," she said.

"What's not?"

She pointed at the two restrooms. "I had to wait like ten minutes, and you get in right away."

"What do you want me to say?"

"That you're sorry."

"For being a man?"

Erika nodded. "Men design these buildings. If they cared about us, maybe they'd put in twice as many stalls for women."

"Maybe a woman with a strong bladder and a well-defined sense of fairness designed this building."

She rolled her eyes. "Please."

I grabbed her hand and headed toward the exit.

From behind me, she said, "Say it."

"That I'm sorry?"

"Yes."

"Why do I have to apologize for something I didn't do?"

"Somebody should say it."

She didn't sound as committed to the argument now that we were walking. I didn't respond to her as we stepped outside. The heat of the day seemed oppressive after being inside the cool building.

"C'mon. Say it."

Glancing back at her, I said, "Yeah, whatever. I'm sorry."

"You don't sound like you mean it."

"Oh, I mean it. Trust me."

She tugged on my hand and turned me around. "What are you sorry for?"

"For the thing." I lifted my chin toward the plaza. "You know."

Her brow furrowed. "You're not sorry."

I laughed and led her back to where Balls Deep and Four Twenty were in the final throes of their game. The score was 19-10.

Bone was on the court now. He bounce-passed the ball to Squirrel, who dunked it. He hollered when he landed. The woman at the scorer's table flipped over the red card. Balls Deep won 20-10.

I said, "They're in the red jerseys."

"I can read their monikers."

"Nicknames."

"Moniker sounds so much more official. I like it. I see why you use it."

After shaking hands with the other team, Carlton Winfrey's friends huddled together and gathered their gear. Each of them carried a red gym bag. A couple of young women, one black and one Hispanic, moved about them with intense interest.

Bone eyed the girls with scorn, then stepped onto the sidewalk. The rest of the group followed. Squirrel dribbled a basketball and brought up the rear.

Erika and I dropped in behind the Dead Boys as they headed over to the concession stand near Riverfront Park's main entrance. Bumps reached into his bag and pulled out a wad of bills. He peeled several off and handed them to the Hispanic woman. The two women then hurried over to a hamburger stand while the guys spread out on a section of grass.

I leaned into Erika. "Would you eavesdrop on the women?"

"I need some money."

"For?"

"If they're getting a snack, I want one."

I smirked and handed her a twenty. She laughed as she headed toward the concession stand.

Bone found a patch of grass and lay with his head on his gym bag. Bumps and Squirrel watched the two women at the concession stand. Grouch eyed any attractive female that walked by.

I kept my hands where they could see them and approached. The same fear I felt at the group of teenagers returned. It was four to one—terrible odds. I'd handled that disparity before, but often a gun was on my hip. "Afternoon, gentlemen."

Bone sat upright, and the others turned toward me.

"Can I ask you a couple questions?"

"About?" Bone asked.

"Carlton Winfrey and his wife."

The others moved behind Bone after he rose to his feet. He was several inches taller than me. He tilted his head back and stared down his nose. "You a cop?"

"I'm a private investigator hired by Tina's attorney."

Grouch said, "That bitch should fry for—" but Bone raised his hand to cut him off.

"Just a couple questions," I said. "Then I'll leave."

Bone said, "You think she's innocent, Shaft?"

Grouch flicked his hand in my direction. "This motherfucker can't be Shaft."

"The author of *Shaft* was white," Bumps said.

"Bullshit," Grouch snapped.

"Yeah," Squirrel said. "Bumps and his bullshit."

Bumps seemed offended. "It's bullshit because I read?"

"You three," Bone growled. "Shut it." The leader of the Dead Boys eyed me. "Back to my question—you think she's innocent?"

I said, "I do."

Bone stepped closer. "What proof you got?"

"That's what I'm working on."

Bone pressed a finger against my chest. "Your girl did it. The cops caught her. They even got a witness. That's enough to send her to the pen."

"She has an alibi," I said.

Grouch crossed his arms. "Then why is she still in jail?" On his right bicep was a large D. On the left was a large B. *Dead Boys*.

"The alibi is her boyfriend."

Bone lowered his face until his nose touched mine. His breath was hot on my face. "Say that again."

"She had a boyfriend."

I saw the movement and flinched, but his hand was faster than my head. His palm smacked me on the side of the head, and I stumbled back.

Why wasn't Bone charging after me? Instead, he simply stood in place and watched me. His lack of additional attack seemed to confuse his partners. They anxiously shifted as if they should be hitting me, too.

Then the choice of the open-handed strike registered. Why had he hit me with that as opposed to a closed-fisted one? I'd certainly hit a man with a fist over a slap if I wanted to make a point.

Around us, a crowd began to watch.

I lifted my hands to a submissive position.

"Where's this boyfriend?"

"The cops have him now."

Bone's tongue darted over his lips. "So, they're setting Tina free?"

"No."

"Why not?"

"She lied to protect the man."

Bone's brow furrowed. He seemed genuinely confused. "Why would she do that?"

"He had a warrant, and she was afraid of this." I waved at him and his friends. "Afraid of what you all might do to her."

Grouch said, "Fuck her, man. And fuck you, too."

Squirrel puffed his chest. "What Grouch said."

Without further word, Bone slowly headed back to his spot on the grass.

Bumps jerked his head toward the street. "You heard the man. Get gone."

"Wait," I said.

Bone looked back as he lowered himself to the ground.

I asked, "Don't you want Carlton's killer found?"

"They already found her," Grouch said.

Squirrel added, "Yeah." It seemed he was thinking about adding something else but couldn't come up with it. So, he just said, "Yeah," a second time.

"Good one," Bumps muttered. Squirrel smacked him with the back of his hand.

"They've got the wrong person," I said. "Since Carlton was your friend, I figured you'd want them to find the right person."

Bone studied me from his place on the grass.

Grouch said, "Hey, man, the bitch did it. We know it. The cops know it."

"How can you be sure?"

"Because Carlton was set to divorce her ass. He'd gotten tired of being tied down."

I eyed Bone, but he was content to let the others speak for him.

Grouch seemed comfortable in the number two position. "It's a crazy world for ballplayers."

"Crazy," Bumps echoed.

"Women threw themselves at him in every city he went to. A wife has got to understand that."

Squirrel laughed. "Don't hate the player. Hate the

game."

Grouch said, "Shut up, Squirrel."

Bone rested on his elbows but continued to remain silent.

I asked, "If he was cheating on Tina, why get mad that she was doing the same?"

Grouch turned to Bumps and Squirrel. "Is this guy serious?" Facing me again, he rubbed his fingers together. "He who makes the bread makes the rules."

Bumps looked toward the concession stand. "Carlton put a roof over her head and shoes on her feet."

"She had nice feet," Squirrel said. Realizing he said something too personal, he said, "Shoes. I meant she had nice shoes."

Grouch shook his head. "All she had to do was spend money and occasionally service my boy. Playing around was his prerogative—not hers."

"Can you think of anyone else who might want Carlton dead?"

"Nope," Grouch said. "Just your girl."

"The cops think you were using him to get access to the majors."

The standing Dead Boys burst into laughter.

Bone asked, "How does Tina know you?"

This question stopped the hysterics, and the three men turned to watch their leader.

I said, "Her attorney hired me."

"You know too much about us and too much about the cops."

Squirrel jumped excitedly. "Her ex-husband was a cop."

Bone's fingers formed a gun, and he pointed it at me. "Are you friends with the ex?"

I avoided the question. "I'm working to establish an alibi."

Grouch grunted. "By pointing the blame at us."

"No, I'm trying—"

He shoved me. "Man, get the fuck outta here."

"Maybe the crew down south were unhappy that Carlton wasn't willing to play ball."

Bone jumped to his feet, and I backpedaled. "You think we killed him?" The others grabbed their leader this time.

"I didn't say that."

Grouch and Bone exchanged a glance. The number two chose his following words carefully. "Carlton was no angel."

"What's that mean?"

"It means," Bone said, "that some of the old crew hated him for leaving the neighborhood. And some of the younger dogs didn't like him sniffing around the neighborhood. It made them nervous. They thought he might be a narc."

"Why have him around then?"

"He's famous, yo," Squirrel said.

Grouch eyed the tall man until Squirrel looked contrite. Then he said, "Carlton ran with us back in the day. He didn't forget where he came from, and we didn't forget him."

Bone said, "We're done. Don't come back again."

Erika trailed several feet behind the women as they arrived with bags of hamburgers. Grouch took their lunch and sat with Bone. Bumps kissed the Hispanic girl, and the black girl ran to Squirrel.

None of them acknowledged I was there anymore. It was official. I had been dismissed.

***

We waited until we were in the thickest portion of the crowd and sure that the Dead Boys weren't following us before we started talking. I held her hand as I led the way back to the truck.

From behind, Erika asked, "How did it go?"

"Not well."

"What happened?"

"They think Tina did it."

"And?"

I glanced over my shoulder. "I couldn't change their minds."

"What did you expect?" We moved around a slow-moving family and into a clear stretch of sidewalk. Erika trotted to my side. "They feel like the cops have got their woman. Case closed."

She was probably right, but I still felt disappointed. I wanted to get something useful from the Dead Boys. However, it did seem like Bone might say something. Maybe if there was a chance to get him alone, he'd feel freer to talk.

"What about you?" I asked. "Did you overhear anything interesting?"

"Those two are nasty."

I raised an eyebrow.

"They compared notes. The Hispanic girl told secrets about JayJay while the other one was dishing dirt about Andre. You don't want to know what they were talking about." Erika shook her head. "Nasty."

We walked in silence for a block, each lost in our respective thoughts.

"What are we going to do now?" she asked.

"There's not much time before the shift tonight. Maybe we can make another run out to Coeur d'Alene."

"For?"

"To see if we can find Mike."

She shrugged. "You don't need me for that."

I fell silent. I wasn't sure if she was about to argue about looking for him, but she'd already helped me look for Mike earlier.

"Unless you want me to go," she added unenthusiastically.

"No, it's cool."

"I want to grab a shower and catch up on some homework. Some of us aren't getting paid for this."

"I could pay you."

"You couldn't afford me."

Chapter 16

After dropping Erika at her car, I headed toward Coeur d'Alene. Besides stopping in at Mike's hotel once more, I had another lead I could follow up on. Carlton Winfrey's murder rolled around in my head during the thirty-minute drive, and I tried to put things in order.

I still believed Tina wasn't involved in her husband's murder. Maybe her marriage hadn't been perfect, but she'd grown comfortable. She was willing to live with Carlton's out-of-town dalliances and the occasional bouts of domestic violence. Human beings are adaptable creatures and capable of living in dire situations.

The cops had already cleared Mike. They had information that I didn't, so I'd go with their judgment. Though maybe they made a mistake. If I was willing to believe the cops made an error in arresting Tina, I had to believe another mistake might have been made in clearing my former friend. The police hadn't heard his racist outbursts. If I hadn't, I don't think I would even consider him a possibility in the murder. But now? I would go with what the cops thought, yet leave the door open to the chance he was involved.

Then there were the Dead Boys. The talk we had in the park didn't go as well as I had hoped. They all seemed content to believe that Tina did it. Any one of them might have information critical to her defense, but they weren't likely to share it with me—definitely not while in a group setting.

And finally, there was Rembrandt Easton—the guy

who was now incarcerated along with Tina. They should have been alibis for each other, but Tina's lie along with Rembrandt's robbery warrant negated their believability.

Beyond the lies and warrant, other things were going against Tina and Rembrandt. The time of their rendezvous was suspect. Five in the morning seemed a strange time for a booty call. However, when a person is involved in a domestic violence situation and afraid of losing her life of comfort, maybe she resorted to odd-timed hook-ups.

And Rembrandt didn't seem Tina's type. He was a skinny artist. Mike was an aggressive cop who lifted weights to stay in shape, and Carlton Winfrey was a professional ballplayer.

Tina and Rembrandt might have been snuggling at five in the morning of Carlton's murder, but a jury was likely to believe the existence of the Easter Bunny before that.

I was to Post Falls, Idaho, before I consciously realized where I was. I had zoned out for almost twenty minutes, circling back and forth on Carlton's murder and Tina's predicament.

A red Mitsubishi Eclipse raced by as if my truck were standing still. It zoomed around the bend and was out of sight.

The image of the red car lingered in my mind. Tina's car—the Jaguar—was red. It should have been in the resort's parking lot, yet Olivia Wagner saw it in the driveway of the Winfrey home. Tina's freedom hinged on those conflicting stories. How could that have happened?

There were three possible explanations.

First, Tina was lying. She never left the house and murdered Carlton, as the cops had theorized. This conflicted with what Rembrandt Easton told me about their morning rendezvous. He could have been lying, too.

The second possible explanation was that Tina drove to the hotel and hooked up with Rembrandt. While there, someone stole her car and returned to her home so they could murder Carlton. Why would the murderer need the vehicle? To frame Tina, but it seemed a complicated reason. Maybe there was a garage door opener inside the car, which could get the murderer into the house. Or perhaps they needed the car keys, which would have a house key on the ring. Which would mean the murderer stole the keys somehow. Maybe Rembrandt gave the car keys to a partner while he entertained Tina. Or was the valet working at that time?

This avenue of reasoning seemed overly complicated.

Olivia Wagner lied was the final explanation for Tina's car being in the driveway. She seemed credible enough, although something *was* off there. With the anniversary of her father's death, she seemed distracted. Maybe the lie wasn't purposeful, though. Perhaps she saw another red car and assumed that it was Tina's Jaguar. Whether it was an intentional lie or an unintentional error, it had double the impact when it was added to Tina's falsehoods.

One thing I hadn't considered yet was the profit in the murder. What would killing Carlton Winfrey get Tina? What would it get Rembrandt Easton? Besides the obvious of freeing them to be together, it was something worth looking into.

I stopped at Mike's hotel. I could have called but figured a personal touch might go a bit further.

The desk clerk I spoke with the day before was still there. He appeared frazzled, no doubt because the hotel was booked with Hoopfest attendees.

"How's it going?" I asked.

He considered me with suspicion. "How may I help

you?"

"Is Mike Davoli still registered here?"

His mistrust faded and was replaced by professionalism. We were now on familiar footing. "I cannot tell you that, sir. It's against company policy. Have a nice day."

"Can you tell me if you've seen him today?"

"We don't share information on our guests. Have a nice day."

I wanted to tell him that he or someone else shared information with my girlfriend earlier this morning, but instead, I only smiled. "More flies with honey."

His brow furrowed.

Outside in my truck, I checked the usable minutes on my phone. I still had about ten left. I would need to reload them soon. The call was answered on the third ring. After telling the receptionist who I was, she put me through to Butch Hollingshead.

"John, what have you learned?"

"Not much. Have you heard from Mike?"

"I take it you haven't either."

"No. I'm getting concerned."

"About him or what he might do to Tina's case?"

"Both."

"You're not making me feel better. If either of us hears from him, let's update the other."

***

Scott Fairchild lived in a neighborhood that abutted Coeur d'Alene's public golf course. The split-level house was painted white with dark brown trim. A two-car garage was attached at the east end, and a trailer with two snowmobiles rested in its driveway. A red cedar fence ran around the rear of the property.

I knocked on the front door and waited.

The front lawn appeared freshly cut, and a lawn mower buzzed in the neighborhood. The more I listened to the whirring motor, the more convinced I became that it emanated from the backyard.

A gate was near the garage, and I simply walked through.

In the furthest portion of the yard, a well-built man in blue shorts and running shoes with no socks pushed a lawnmower. His back and broad shoulders glistened with sweat.

It didn't take long for him to notice me. He stopped pushing, and the mower fell silent.

"What is it?" he called out.

I walked toward him. "Sorry to bother you. I'm John Cutler."

He dropped his head for a moment as if trying to recollect my name. When he looked up, he said, "You're the guy who talked with Olivia."

"That's correct." I stopped walking and stood in the middle of the yard.

"What do you want?" Hostility laced his question.

"Just a couple questions."

"I wasn't there, and I never met those people."

The way he said *those people* was all the hint I needed. I knew I'd been viewing things lately through a lens of racism, but there was no mistaking where he stood.

Fairchild walked by me on his way toward the house. I didn't bother to offer my hand. Neither did he. When he made it to the deck, he ascended the stairs. He grabbed a beer bottle from a small table and took a long swig. "What is it you think I can tell you?"

I moved toward the deck. "I want to learn a little more about Olivia."

He pointed the bottle down at me. "You've got the wrong guy if you want me to trash her for some mud shark."

The slur rolled off his tongue without a hint of embarrassment. Getting into an argument with him wasn't going to get any information. Maybe the perceived power imbalance—him standing above me—allowed him to think it was okay to speak this way. I moved around to the deck stairs. Still looking up at him, I said, "Has she said anything about her neighbors?"

His face scrunched. "Why would she?"

I ascended the stairs. "A man was murdered."

Fairchild absently waved his beer. "She'll get over it."

"Most people seem to take that experience sort of hard."

He sniffed dismissively.

"But you don't think so."

Fairchild hesitated to respond. Now that I was on the deck, we stood at eye level. He didn't seem as willing to spout off. Maybe he sensed my feelings for him.

"She's got other things on her mind," he finally said. "Her father died last year. And we're getting married in Hawaii. She's handling the arrangements."

"That's a lot of work."

"Olivia's a smart gal. She's got it under control." His brow furrowed. "Why are you talking to me exactly?"

I thought about mentioning the strange vibe Olivia gave concerning him, but the woman had been somewhat forthcoming. I didn't see a reason to create a problem to blow back on her. "Where were you the morning Carlton Winfrey was murdered?"

Fairchild smiled. "You don't honestly think."

"I don't know. That's why I'm asking."

He cast a sideways glance before reluctantly answering. "I was flying back from a golf trip to Pebble Beach, and, no, I'm not showing you proof of my trip. Besides, if I want to kill that porch—"

I shoved him, and he stumbled into the small table. It fell over and banged onto the decking.

"The hell, man?" He stepped forward now, but it was only for show—a bully maneuver. He didn't come any closer.

"Watch your mouth."

"This is my house. I can say any damn thing I want."

"You're right." I stepped back. "It is your house, but I don't have to listen to you."

As I turned to leave, he said, "It's guys like you who are giving our country to them."

I stopped and faced him.

He pointed behind me. "Get off my porch."

"Say it again."

"You need to go."

I stepped forward. "Come on, tough guy. Say it again."

Scott Fairchild let his beer bottle slip through his fingers until he gripped it only by the neck. Now he held a little glass club in his hand. "Leave." He didn't sound so tough now.

"That's what I thought. Nothing but a bitch."

He reared back with the beer bottle, but I punched him. The beer bottle flew from his hand and landed in the yard somewhere. He collapsed awkwardly to the deck. The side of his head hit the deck and sounded like a watermelon dropped from six feet. Scott Fairchild wasn't getting back up. The humane thing to do would have been to check on him.

Instead, I left the man there and walked back to my truck.

Chapter 17

The failed interview with Scott Fairchild went faster than expected, so I still had plenty of time before my shift at Club Royale. I detoured to the Kootenai County Jail to see if I could visit Tina again.

"You're back." She didn't smile.

"Carlton's crew doesn't like you."

"Tell me something I don't know."

"They're upset about you stepping out on your husband."

Her face flattened. "You told them about Rembrandt? Why would you do that?"

"I didn't tell them his name, but I said you had a boyfriend."

"Oh, shit." She rolled her eyes. "They had to love that."

"They didn't."

"It's part of their macho bullshit. Carlton could run around and do what he did, but I had to stay home and play the loyal wife."

"You signed on for it."

"I signed on for it because he was handsome and charming. Maybe some of it had to do with him being a younger man. At times, I think he liked it when I mothered him."

"But you knew about the other women?"

"I'm not an idiot, John. Of course, I knew. He was a major league ballplayer. Even when he was in the minors, women were around all the time."

"Did you know he was filing for divorce?"

She looked down at her hands. "Not until Butch told me about it, but I thought he might. You kind of sense when that stuff is coming."

"Why do you think he wanted the divorce?"

Tina's eyes returned to mine. "Probably because of me stepping out on him. I told you he suspected it. It wasn't equal footing in our relationship. He could hook up—not me. I violated the unspoken rule."

"The Dead Boys are convinced you killed him."

"I'm not surprised. They couldn't come up with anyone else with a motive?"

"Only you."

She looked away.

"What do you know about Bone?"

"Why do you ask?"

"He seemed… *strange*."

"How so?"

I leaned in. "When I said you had a boyfriend, he hit me. But it wasn't as hard as he could have. I'm sure of that. And when he found out that your boyfriend was arrested, but you weren't released, he seemed surprised. I think he knows more than he's letting on."

"LaShaun's an intense guy. He's smarter than he lets on."

"Did he know about Rembrandt?"

"Not that I know of. Will you talk to him again?"

"Bone? Yeah, I think I have to. What do you know about Olivia Wagner?"

Tina shrugged. "She's the neighbor, right? Butch told me her name. I've never met the woman. Now, I wish I had. Why do you ask?"

"I'm trying to get you out. Looking at everyone I can."

We fell into silence after that. I didn't have a whole lot

of questions for her. I'd only stopped by because of the extra time. "Have you talked to Jaime?"

"Not yet, but Mike said she's doing well."

"Mike? When did you talk with him?"

She squinted. "He came by maybe thirty minutes after you left this morning. He said you guys talked outside." Her face relaxed. "But by that look, I can see that he lied."

"How'd he seem?"

"Rough, like he hadn't gotten any sleep. And he didn't say much, either. Just wanted to check on me, see how I was doing, that sort of thing." She rubbed her hands together. "He didn't sound right."

"How do you mean?"

"He seemed to be drifting when he spoke."

"Was he drunk?"

"I don't think so."

"If he comes back, ask what he's trying to do."

Tina seemed to shrink in her seat. "Do you think he's going to hurt someone?"

"If he thought it would bring you back, he'd burn down the world."

***

After collecting my belongings at the jail's security desk, I powered on my cell phone. A voicemail alert popped up.

"*Hey, John. This is Butch. Listen. I know we just talked, but my buddy from the PA's office called and let me know where to find Carlton Winfrey's friends.*" He then listed the address and the apartment numbers.

Time was getting tight, but I was already in Coeur d'Alene. I could quickly check out the apartments and make it back to Spokane before my shift at the club.

The multi-family community was several blocks long and as many blocks deep. The gray and white buildings were three stories high. Manicured landscaping surrounded the structures.

It was early afternoon, and Balls Deep should still be on a court somewhere in Hoopfest. Apartments B326 and B327 faced each other and shared a small third-floor landing. I knocked on both doors and waited for several minutes. Neither opened.

Heading back toward Spokane, I was almost to the freeway when red and blue lights flashed in the rearview mirror. The speedometer showed twenty-six miles per hour—four under the limit. I continued past the freeway entrance and pulled into the parking lot of a convenience store.

The patrol cruiser followed me in.

I silenced the truck's engine, rolled down my window, and put both hands on the steering wheel. My gun was in the glovebox, along with the vehicle's registration and proof of insurance.

A second patrol car pulled into the parking lot alongside the other. A pit grew in my stomach. Two units were a bad sign and unnecessary for a simple traffic infraction.

A young male officer climbed out of the first patrol car and hesitated to assess the situation. His eyes flicked into the bed of the truck as he walked by. Even though I watched him in the side mirror, he avoided locking onto my eyes. Instead, he searched for any furtive movements I might be making. He stopped at the cab's support beam behind my left shoulder. The officer's safety techniques were textbook sharp.

"Afternoon, sir. I'm Officer Crawley with the Coeur

d'Alene Police Department. May I see your driver's license?" His delivery was practiced and smooth.

"Sure." I dug the wallet from my back pocket and pulled the license free. After handing it to Crawley, I asked, "Why'd you stop me?"

A knock on the opposite window caused me to look away. An older black officer mimed rolling down the window. I lowered that window.

"Where you headed?" the older officer asked with a slow drawl that sounded as if it originated from somewhere other than the Pacific Northwest. His name tag read Jefferson.

Behind me, Crawley ran my name via his portable radio. He phonetically spelled my last name to the dispatcher.

I knew what they were doing—one officer kept me occupied while the other ran my name. I'd played the game before, and it's done when a matter is considered severe. There was only one thing that could have earned me this much attention, and I wasn't going to admit what I had done until forced. But I needed to start laying the groundwork for that admission because it was likely to be discussed.

I said to Officer Jefferson, "I'm headed back to Spokane."

"What brought you to Coeur d'Alene today?"

I removed my investigator's license and extended it to Jefferson. "I'm working a case."

The older officer took the card. "Private eye, huh? Couldn't make it through the academy?" His tone was mocking but without much conviction. He was only poking me, looking for a reaction, seeing if I might slip up.

"I made the grade."

Jefferson bent to study me closer. "Where at?"

"Seattle. Quit a couple years ago."

"That so?"

Crawley shuffled behind me. He was waiting for the dispatcher to return with the results of my name check.

"Why'd you quit?" Jefferson asked.

Officers who willingly walk away from the job are rare and often treated with a mixture of disbelief and appreciation. Some are seen as getting out with their souls and happiness intact.

Yet, I hadn't willingly walked away. I was kicked out. That's not a unique occurrence, and guys like that are viewed with almost universal disdain. Even if it was an unintentional act, those former officers somehow dirtied the badge. They aren't likely to ever be extended grace.

I needed an answer that straddled the fence between lie and truth. "The job no longer suited me."

"How's that?" Crawley asked.

I glanced over my shoulder then put my eyes back on the older officer. "You wake up one day and find the guy in the mirror isn't the one who graduated the academy. You make a choice at that point. You either work to go back to that guy you once were, or you stay the man you've become."

It was the truth, but still a lie. I hadn't worked to get back to the man who graduated from the academy. That's why the Seattle PD kicked me out.

Officer Jefferson handed back my investigator's card. "You're only licensed in Washington. Got one for Idaho?"

"No, sir." I was extra polite. "I'm working for Butch Hollingshead."

"We know Butch," Jefferson said.

"Unfortunately," Crawley muttered.

"He asked me to help a woman currently suspected of murder."

Crawley asked, "Would that help lead to a Scott Fairchild?"

"Yes, sir," I said, keeping politeness at the forefront of any response. "I talked with Mr. Fairchild."

And that's why I laid the groundwork. Fairchild had called the cops after I knocked him out. I didn't know how the law worked in Idaho, but the Washington equivalent stated that I faced a felony. This wasn't a simple assault. I had knocked Fairchild unconscious. I could try and lie my way out of this, but that would only dig my hole deeper. Earlier, I figured punching Fairchild was worth it. Nothing had changed since.

"What happened?" Jefferson asked.

"May I get out of the truck and explain myself?"

The older office nodded. "By all means."

We walked back toward their patrol cars. Getting out wasn't going to stop them from searching my truck if I was arrested. Instead, I wanted to change the power dynamic. When Scott Fairchild stood over me on the porch, he felt naturally more powerful. I believed the same thing occurred with me sitting in my truck and the two officers standing at both my windows. All I wanted to do was present my story to them in an open manner and build rapport.

Out of habit, my hands slid into my pockets. Jefferson calmly said, "Keep your hands where I can see them."

I pulled them out.

"C'mon," Crawley said. "Let's hear your story."

"Butch Hollingshead represents Carlton Winfrey's wife."

The younger officer snorted. "You're working *that*

case? It's a loser. The wife did it."

"She has an alibi," I said.

Crawley chuckled. "The boyfriend? I was there when we arrested him. That's not an alibi. That's a nail in her coffin."

Jefferson remained silent and studied me.

"How's Scott Fairchild figure into this?" Crawley asked.

"His fiancée is the witness who placed Tina Winfrey at the scene of the crime that morning."

"Oh, hell," the younger officer said, "now I see it. Hollingshead is planning on putting the witness on trial." He turned to Jefferson. "That sounds like him, doesn't it?"

"Butch didn't send me," I said. "The witness mentioned her fiancé, and she didn't want me talking to him. She seemed worried about it."

Jefferson crossed his arms. "So, what did Fairchild say?"

"Nothing that would help my client."

Another chuckle from Crawley. "Whatever he said must have pissed you off."

I glanced to Jefferson then back to the younger officer. "Is he all right?"

"Bloody nose and a scrape on the side of his head. Claims he lost consciousness."

"Was anyone around to prove that?"

Crawley smirked. "What if there was?"

There wasn't. Now, I was less worried. I could deal with a misdemeanor assault.

Jefferson asked, "What *did* Fairchild say?"

"He talked about the Winfreys in a way I found offensive."

Crawley shook his head. "You just can't hit people

because they say offensive things."

The older officer asked, "Why would *you* find what he said offensive?"

"Besides the usual peace-on-earth stuff?"

"Spare me."

"I did it because of my girlfriend."

Jefferson lifted his eyebrows. I nodded, and he caught my meaning.

"Dating her doesn't give you the right to hit him."

Crawley asked, "Am I missing something?"

"If it did," Jefferson continued, "I would have punched a lot of men through the years." The older officer considered me then. After a while, he decided on something and turned to Crawley. "All we've got is a misdemeanor."

"Cite and release?"

"Let's run that route." Jefferson pointed at the bumper of the first patrol car and said to me, "Put your butt there until we're done."

Crawley slipped into his car. I looked over my shoulder and saw him with his head down, presumably filling out my ticket.

Jefferson stood nearby. Neither of us said anything until Crawley exited the patrol car. He handed me a pen and pointed at a spot on the page.

"You're not admitting guilt," the younger officer said, "you're only signing that you've received the citation and that you promise to appear in court."

After scribbling my signature, I returned the pen.

"Should we search his truck?" Crawley asked.

Jefferson's brow furrowed. "What for?"

"Incident to arrest."

The older office motioned toward the ticket book.

"Give the man his copy, and let's go. We've already invested more time on this than I want to."

The younger officer handed me the citation. "If you fail to appear in court, they'll issue a warrant."

"I understand."

Jefferson said, "Stay out of trouble."

"Yeah," Crawley added. "We don't need you Washingtonians coming over here and making problems for us."

They stayed in their cars until I drove away.

Chapter 18

By ten that night, the line outside Club Royale curled around the far end of the block. About two hundred people waited anxiously to get inside. Even though the club was the hottest joint in town, there was never a line on a typical night. And only major holidays like New Years' and St. Patrick's Day drew lines of about fifty people.

The club's Russian owner, Bosco, didn't mind pushing the occupancy limits, but he didn't dare do such a thing on Hoopfest weekend. Too many liquor control agents, deputy fire marshals, and undercover cops prowled around for him to attempt such a blatant violation. Club Royale had a notorious, if not well-earned, reputation for overcapacity. But doing such a thing tonight would be sticking a thumb in the eye of enforcement. They wouldn't take kindly to such a thing.

Some seasoned bartenders talked about a club losing its liquor license for a month after a repeated over-capacity violation. That bar never recovered and was forced to permanently close—it was the predecessor of Club Royale.

From inside the club, Three 6 Mafia's "Stay Fly" thumped loudly.

Some teenagers played at one of the hoops in the middle of the street. It wasn't uncommon to find evening games going on around downtown over the weekend. The temperatures were cooler, and the streetlights provided enough illumination. It was an experience that most Spokanites would never get. The folks waiting in line cheered the players on.

"Two out," a voice came through my earpiece. For the event weekend, the security staff wore radio headsets to communicate. I motioned forward an attractive black couple. They both extended their IDs.

"I hear this is the place," the boyfriend said.

I nodded. Normally, I'd engage in idle banter, but tonight was about being hyper-observant. Further down the line, two women danced with each other too enthusiastically. That usually meant one thing—they were already intoxicated.

"Or the Double Dribble," the girlfriend added. "People are saying that's the other one we should check out."

My attention returned to the couple's licenses. They were from out-of-state, and I wasn't familiar with their cards, but there were still things I could do to verify them. First, I waved a black-light pen over the document. A holographic symbol shone back. That was only the first step in confirming authenticity.

The boyfriend said, "I heard the Dribble's rough."

"But they supposedly got the better service."

That caught my attention.

The boyfriend nervously laughed. "She didn't mean nothing by that."

I shrugged and ran my thumb over both cards. As a cop and as a bouncer, I'd experienced times when one party was of legal age and their partner wasn't. Neither card had damage, and they felt real. Fake IDs feel like laminated paper. They'll hold up to the eye test but touch them for any length of time, and their phoniness will be revealed.

Lastly, I held the cards up to verify the pictures were of the individuals in front of me. One of the easiest ways to get a fake ID is to borrow a valid one from an of-age friend.

The photos checked out.

If I remained worried, I could have asked them their birthdays and worked the math. However, I was convinced the couple matched their IDs and were of legal age. I handed back their cards, motioned them inside, and clicked the add button on my tally counter.

I was responsible for managing the club's exterior. That meant checking IDs before sending customers into the foyer to pay their cover and ensuring we stayed close to capacity—a little over was acceptable.

Enforcement officials can't count the exact number, and I've learned that there's visually little difference between eight and nine hundred people. Get over a thousand, though, and it was like a red flag. Bosco liked when I ran the door because he knew I gamed the system, but I'm not lax while doing so.

I worked the inside on a New Year's Eve when someone careless handled the door. The crowd grew so large it took on a rhythm of its own. When Bosco and I realized what had happened, it was too late. He and I were in the middle of the crowd when it swelled unexpectantly. We were pushed five feet in one direction, then the mob pulled back and jerked us in the opposite. Cheers and hollers of excitement came from the throng. When we shoved our way through the mass of people, Bosco fired the doorman on the spot.

We knew the enforcement officials were on the prowl and had to make an emergency decision or face a license suspension. He closed the club immediately and refunded everyone their cover. That experience left him with a new sense of respect for the doorman. Since then, I get bonused for getting the club through event nights without a warning from the enforcement agencies.

Even though the rear doorman hadn't announced anyone left, I waved forward the next couple. This was the art of managing overcapacity. I had a separate count in my head of how many extra people I'd let in. Sixty so far. That meant forty more could get in, and I'd still feel comfortable with enforcement officials walking through.

The regular cover charge was five bucks per person. On Hoopfest weekend, it was raised to ten. Anyone willing to pay twenty-five dollars could jump to the front. Bosco loved the idea of capitalism and embraced the law of supply and demand. He somehow determined that the club turned over entirely at least twice on Hoopfest Saturday. Since the club's occupancy limit is eight hundred people, he collected sixteen grand without selling a single drink.

Everyone knew that Club Royale was *the* place to be. By eleven o'clock, we would tell people at the back of the line that they wouldn't get in.

Bosco appeared at my shoulder. "It is good tonight."

"Not bad."

Even though he wore a headset, Bosco preferred to see things for himself. That attitude was why his club continued to thrive while new clubs often flamed out.

"It was hot today," I said. "Lots of sunburned faces in the crowd."

"So?"

"Dehydrated folks inside. Angry players who lost, too. Be alert."

Bosco clapped my shoulder. "You always worry about my business, John. That is why I like you."

The big Russian waved the two drunk twenty-somethings forward. They were dressed for trouble—tight miniskirts, high heels, too much makeup. They shimmied as they walked.

Inside the club, Christina Milian's "Dip It Low" pounded.

The women held out their ID cards, but I refused to take them.

"You're overserved. Step out of line."

The two glanced at each other and appeared ready to argue, but Bosco intervened. "No, no. There must be some mistake."

This cheered up the women.

"Come with me," Bosco said. "You have your cover, no?"

Even when he was flirting, Bosco made sure to put his capitalism face forward. The three of them disappeared inside.

I recognized four faces in line halfway down the block. Andre "Squirrel" Murphy and JayJay "Bumps" Robinson stood with their girlfriends. Squirrel looked sharp in a white silk shirt and black slacks. On the other hand, Bumps looked overdressed in a dark purple suit with a shirt of the same color. The ladies wore short silver skirts that highlighted their long legs.

The men whispered to each other and looked about furtively. The women didn't seem to care that Squirrel and Bumps were ignoring them. They were engaged in a private conversation of their own.

I kept my eye on the four as the line slowly moved. Not many were leaving per the guy manning the exit, but I still allowed a couple of customers to slip in occasionally. My overcapacity number was approaching one hundred.

When they were about fifteen feet from the door, Squirrel noticed me. The left side of his face was bruised and swollen. He smacked Bumps with the back of his hand. When the heavyset man turned my way, his smile faded.

The music inside changed again. This time it was Dirty Vegas' annoyingly poppy "Days Gone By." The crowd nearest the door moved along with the electronic rhythm.

From behind, a familiar voice said, "Hey, man."

I turned to find Mike Davoli standing there.

"Where the hell have you been?" I asked.

"Around."

"Doing what?"

"What do you think?"

It was then I noticed his blackened right eye and cut lip.

I whirled around to check the line. Squirrel and Bumps were gone. So were their girls. Facing Mike, I pointed down the block away from the line. "Wait over there. I'll be with you in a few."

After requesting a replacement, it took only a minute for one to step outside and cover my post.

As I approached Mike, I said, "You look like shit."

"You should see the other guy."

"I did."

His brow furrowed. "For real? Andre was here?" He looked toward the line.

"Along with Bumps."

"Fucking monikers. Makes them sound like *The Little Rascals*."

"Why are you here?"

His gaze returned to me. "Tina said this is where you'd be." He looked at the line then grimaced. "You like this music?"

"Most of it."

He flicked his hand. "I remember."

"So, what did you do to Squirrel and Bumps?"

"I didn't do anything to that fat fuck, but I tuned

Squirrel up."

"Why?"

"He wasn't talking."

"You didn't need to do that."

"The hell, I didn't."

I eyed him.

"Are you seriously pissed off that I tuned up some—" He paused. I wasn't sure if he was looking for a politer way to insult an entire race or if he were simply working up the bravery to say a pejorative term in front of this club.

Through clenched teeth, I said, "Don't say it."

"Hell, John, bangers aren't citizens. They get what they get."

That sentiment—they get what they get—was a popular refrain while I was on the police department. I'd said it myself. By their actions, criminals earned the negative karma the universe sent their way. As officers, we were happy to be the delivery system of that justice.

I rubbed my face. "Well?"

"Well, what?"

"Did Squirrel tell you anything?"

"To go fuck myself."

"You catch more flies with honey."

He smirked. "You're giving me advice on how to treat them? May I remind you that you got kicked off the department for what you did."

"It's not the same."

Mike laughed. "It's not? Tell me you didn't beat down that man."

"It didn't happen like that."

"You're lucky you didn't get arrested for violating his civil rights."

I cocked my head. "What is your problem?"

Mike stiffened and motioned behind me.

With a glance over my shoulder, I saw her. Erika stood at the edge of the sidewalk with a cup of something and a Styrofoam container.

"I brought a snack," she muttered. Her gaze shifted to Mike. "What's he talking about?"

"Nothing."

"You violated someone's civil rights?"

Mike stepped forward. "I was being a dick. Just popping off. Don't listen to any of the shit I say."

Her eyes told the truth—she didn't believe his explanation.

I stepped forward. "Erika—"

From down the street, an engine revved. A black Escalade with tinted windows raced in our direction. It sped along the edge of the sidewalk since the middle of the street was blocked off with the basketball hoops.

"What the hell?" Mike muttered.

Erika faced the oncoming vehicle.

The SUV slowed, and a gun extended from the back seat as it neared.

"Down!" I yelled and dove for Erika. I hit her like a linebacker blindsides a quarterback. The container and the cup went flying.

The gun fired several times, and several people screamed.

In my ear, the rear doorman shouted, "Gun! Gun!"

I didn't get up. I stayed on top of Erika. My hands and arms desperately tried to encapsulate her underneath me.

There were screams until the SUV roared away.

It was over in seconds, but it felt like year-long minutes.

Pushing myself up, I got a better look at Erika. She stared at me with wide eyes.

There was so much radio chatter in my ear that I pulled the headset free and let it dangle.

"Are you okay?" I asked.

Erika nodded.

"Did I hurt you?"

Tears welled in her eyes.

"I'm sorry."

Her arms wrapped around me, and she pulled me down. She shivered for several moments. Neither of us said anything.

"I've got to get up," I said.

Her grip released. I kissed her gently on the forehead then stood.

No one was in the line now. Everyone had scattered for safety.

It seemed an odd sight, but the Styrofoam container lay open nearby. Inside, a sandwich had exploded. The kitchen was closed tonight. Erika must have made it for me. It was a loving gesture and a silly thing to be focused on now. Water leaked from the cup.

"Oh my God!" a woman screamed.

I spun.

Mike Davoli lay face down on the sidewalk.

Chapter 19

Major Crimes Detective Gary Ackerman arrived at the club almost forty minutes after the shooting. He spoke with the on-scene officers, then carefully surveyed the scene. When he saw me, he waved once. I motioned back. Then Ackerman continued to wander about. From where I sat across the street, it looked aimless. I'm sure it was anything but.

In the academy, they taught how to approach a crime scene—slowly and from the outside in. Ackerman seemed to be making a bit of a zigzag pattern, but I couldn't be sure. His hands were in his pockets. Officers rarely did this, but detectives didn't have the same worry about safety. The scene was already locked down, so no one was likely to jump him. Maybe the hands were tucked into the pockets so he wouldn't be tempted to touch anything.

Mike's body lay exposed to the night elements. A sheet only covered a body in the movies.

Cops—both uniformed and those in plain clothes—were everywhere. I figured those in jeans and t-shirts were the gang unit. They carried a demeanor of permanent hostility.

Erika and I were separated after the scene was secured. Rationally, I understood it. The responding officers didn't want our recollections of the event to cross-contaminate. Emotionally, though, it pissed me off.

I wanted to talk with her. Not only to calm her down after the shooting but to explain what she might have heard Mike say. I *had* assaulted a black man while in Seattle, and it was one of the contributing factors that led to my termination. It had nothing to do with the man's skin color but everything to do with my feelings toward Paige. I'm not sure I'd tell Erika about her, but I would admit being a loose cannon then.

The longer Erika sat with the crap Mike spouted off, the harder it would be to defend myself. Unfortunately, I could no longer see her. She had been sitting about thirty feet away. A uniform had moved her somewhere else.

Ackerman stepped off the sidewalk and crossed the street. With a slight grunt, he joined me on the curb. "Long time, no see."

I nodded.

"Still got the dog?"

Another nod.

"Did you know the victim?"

"Yeah."

"A friend?"

"Not so much."

Ackerman cast a sideways glance.

"He was my partner."

"In Seattle?"

I nodded again.

"Was this because of the job?"

"No."

"And not random?"

"No."

"Who did it?"

"It's a long story."

"I'm on the clock," Ackerman said. "I like long stories."

I laid it out. Starting from the moment Mike arrived at my house until the shooting. I even told him about getting arrested in Coeur d'Alene.

"And you don't think there's a chance it could be anyone else?"

"Who else could it be?"

"It's Hoopfest weekend, John. Weird stuff goes on at night."

"It's them," I said.

"Did you see the shooters?"

I shook my head.

"Too bad. The only description we've got from the other witnesses is two black males."

"A lot of people around for nobody to see nothing."

He smirked. "You didn't see anything."

"I was face down on the concrete, protecting my girlfriend. Where is she, by the way?"

Ackerman looked around. "Which one is she?"

"You know."

He turned back. "Gang unit is talking to her."

"Why?"

"To see if she saw anything."

"We already said she didn't."

"We?"

"She." My face warmed, and anger rose in my chest.

Ackerman must have sensed it. "What's wrong?"

"It's because she's black."

"The hell are you talking about?"

I looked away. I didn't know what I was talking about. Ackerman was a good guy. He didn't need me seeing ghosts.

"They're re-interviewing her because you guys were less than ten feet from a homicide. They'll re-interview you, too."

"Right."

Ackerman leaned toward me. "Ever think you might be in shock?"

"Huh?"

"Look around, John. This was a critical incident. A man died. Maybe your body is sending you some signals about it."

"I'm fine."

"Sure, you are."

A thought occurred to me, and I faced him. "The Dead Boys."

Ackerman cocked his head. "What about them?"

"Murphy and Robinson—Squirrel and Bumps—besides their buddies in Coeur d'Alene, maybe there's a local connection they could hook up with."

The detective nodded. "I'll let the gang unit know."

A plainclothes officer escorted Erika in our direction. Her arms were crossed, and she looked frightened.

"Or you can let them know," Ackerman said. "Looks like they want to talk with you now."

The pale officer said, "You're free to go, ma'am. Thank you for your statement." To me, he said, "Mr. Cutler, if you'll follow me."

I stood and reached for Erika. She kept her arms tightly around herself.

"Hey."

She stared at me.

From behind, Ackerman said, "I'll catch up with you later, John."

I didn't look back.

The officer cleared his throat. "Mr. Cutler, if you would."

Erika said, "I'll wait for you," and sat.

I touched her shoulder and kissed the top of her head.

She stiffened when I did so.

As I followed the gang-unit officer to where he expected to interview me, I couldn't help but feel that something had irreparably broken between Erika and me.

***

We lay in the darkness, shoulder to shoulder, still in our clothes. Six inches of space was between us, but we couldn't have been further apart. Corporal slept at the foot of the bed, and the fan whirred from the corner of the room.

"Have you ever said those words?" she asked.

I immediately knew the ones she referenced. For a moment, I thought about asking which she meant. "No."

"You're sure?"

"I'm being honest."

Silence descended again and hung over the room. The dog snored. I fought the desire to say something—anything—just to end the quiet. Doing so might be the crack in the dam that would bring forth a torrent of emotions. I didn't want that either. Better to let it remain dammed up until we could get beyond this moment. I wanted to sleep—to wake up in the morning and start over. Not necessarily fresh, but with a clearer perspective. I was too tired and wrung out to make sense.

"You have no idea what's it like to grow up with those words." Her hand balled into a fist. "People you're close to will say stupid things. Things like she's my black friend. I'm dating a black girl." She faced me. "Do you say that about me? That you're dating a black woman?"

"Never."

Even in the low light, she studied me for too long. When her gaze returned to the ceiling, she said, "Those are the nice things they say."

Her hand relaxed, then balled again. It was as if she were trying to work out her demons through that simple motion.

"I've been called well-spoken by older, white women. Did they think I was going to be illiterate? Why would they think that?"

I thought about Erin. My daughter would face hurdles in life because of her gender, but she would avoid the added weight that skin color brought.

"Security guards have followed me around a store. Do you know how embarrassing that is? How demoralizing? They didn't know me. They knew my color. You've met my parents. I'm as likely to steal something as I am to join the NRA."

There was nothing to say at that moment. I had never experienced anything like that. I tried to empathize with her, but I hated that all I could come up with was how I felt when I approached the Dead Boys. Rationally, I explained away that blast of emotion as four against one, but was it because it was four black men against one white man? Would I have felt the same if it were four white men versus me? I thought I would, but now there was a lingering doubt.

"Men in cars have yelled 'Go back to Africa' when I'm on the sidewalk." Tears ran down the side of her face. "I was born here. This is my home."

I touched her hand, but it remained balled in a fist.

She cried softly for several minutes.

There hadn't been a right time to say the words. Would there ever be the perfect moment? I needed her to know how I felt. "I love you."

Erika faced me, and her face pinched.

"I mean it."

She rolled out of bed and stood. The dog alerted and jumped to his feet.

I propped up on an elbow. "Where are you going?"

"Home."

"But I said—"

"Now?" She lifted her hands and bit back her words. "I can't even."

She walked out of the bedroom.

"Erika." I followed her through the kitchen into the living room.

The dog trotted to catch up with her. She burst through the screen door, and it slammed shut behind her.

Both Corporal and I watched as her car disappeared from the neighborhood.

Chapter 20

I called Butch Hollingshead's cell phone in the morning and brought him up to speed.

"And you think," Butch said, "that Mr. Winfrey's friends are responsible for Mike's murder?"

"I do."

He sighed. "I'll let her know."

"Thank you."

"Can you come by today? I want to get an update on Tina's investigation and see where else we might be able to poke."

"I'll see what I can do," I said. "I've got some personal things to attend to."

He hung up without saying goodbye.

After that, the dog and I went for a walk. We meandered down Pettet Drive toward the Spokane River. As we walked, I tried to deal with my thoughts concerning Mike Davoli. Occasionally, I talked to the dog like he was part friend, part psychologist.

"Stupid son of a bitch brought it on himself."

Mike assaulted Squirrel Murphy. I would never know what he learned, but either that information or just the beating itself killed him.

While we were on the department together, I thought of us as brothers—like family. When Tina left him for Carlton, Mike fell apart. I helped put him back together. When my world fell apart, Mike tried to help, but I refused. Everything crashed and burned around me. I left everything behind, including him.

"He wasn't always like he was." Corporal ignored me and chose to sniff a crumpled candy wrapper. "Maybe he was an asshole, but he wasn't a bigot."

Mike loved Tina, but he'd taken her for granted. I'd witnessed it. The little jokes about her. The missed family time. The extra-duty shifts. When Tina's disillusionment led her to a younger, handsome man who paid attention, Mike didn't stand a chance.

"Maybe I dodged a bullet not getting married." Corporal wagged his tail. "Hey, are you listening to me?" He pulled on his leash and yanked my arm. A squirrel darted across the street.

I'd only asked one woman to get married, but she refused. I made the offer after Maria found out she was pregnant. It seemed the right thing to do. But the proposal wasn't from love—it was out of obligation. Maybe Victorian-era marriage would last out of duty, but a modern marriage was doomed if built only on that. Maria knew that.

I didn't believe that Erika and I would walk blissfully through life. I knew there would be hard times. Yet, I did cherish her. Or was that too strong of a word? Did I take her for granted?

The dog and I found a path toward the river. The water gurgled and bubbled as it flowed by. Corporal watched it with intense curiosity.

It pissed me off that I said those three words last night. Not that I didn't mean them. I'm fairly sure that I did. But I said them out of desperation. I did that with Paige, too.

I waited until things were too far gone before saying how I felt.

***

Around ten, I knocked on the door and wondered the same thing I always did—how much did it cost to get *Taylor* into that wrought iron circle? The door opened, and Lonnie peered through the screen door.

"John," he said. Gone was his typically happy demeanor. "What can I do for you?"

He had to know I was there for Erika. "Can I talk with her?"

"She's not home."

I pointed to her car in the driveway. "C'mon."

His face remained impassive. "She's not here, and if she were, she wouldn't want to talk."

"Please, Lonnie."

"Don't confuse my friendliness with friendship."

My brow furrowed. "She told you about last night?"

"The shooting? Of course, she did. She also told us about your friend."

"That's not me."

"Better not be." Lonnie opened the screen door and stepped outside. I moved back. When he motioned for me to sit next to him on the steps, I did so.

"Erika is idealistic, John. I'd like to say it's her youth, but I'm not sure it will ever leave her."

I didn't say anything, nor did I nod in agreement. I wasn't sure I was to do anything but listen.

Lonnie looked at me from the corner of his eye. "You told her you loved her."

"I did."

He inhaled deeply then let out a long, slow exhale. When he ran out of breath, he shook his head. "Do you know how much pressure Erika got from seeing you?"

"Some."

"More than you can imagine."

Lonnie cast another sideways glance, but I remained silent. Again, it felt as if I was there to listen.

"Carissa grew up in Alabama. Ever been? No? Well, imagine what it was like in the sixties. Times were tough. Civil rights protests. Anti-war protests. People were demonstrating against the protests. A lot of folks didn't want change." Lonnie ran a finger along the edge of the concrete stair. "Carissa's an attractive woman, but she was a beautiful girl. She could take your breath away. Some men leered at her even though they later called her vile, evil things while in public. Some men who wore badges arrested her younger brother on propped-up charges during the marches. A judge sentenced him to five years in prison for possession of marijuana. He was killed behind bars. Politicians sent her older brother to fight a people he had no beef with. He died in a rice field."

Erika had told me some of this but hearing it from Lonnie—a man of that generation—seemed to carry more weight. I stared at my boots.

"So, you can see why my wife harbors some distrust toward white men. Toward you."

"And you?"

"Honestly?"

No, I didn't want to hear his honest opinion. I liked Lonnie and wanted his approval. If it was anything but, I hoped he would keep it to himself.

"You're an underachiever, John."

The words felt like a well-placed uppercut. My breathing stuttered as I prepared for what followed.

He continued. "You've been to college but left the police department. Okay, fine. Maybe that's not what you were meant to do. Men can change course in their lives.

But what have you done since then? Some odd jobs? Bouncing? You've started an investigation business, and I hope you're successful at it—I really do—but what do you want out of life? As far as I've been able to get from our talks, all you want is to make ends meet. Is that the type of man I want for Erika? And it's got nothing to do with your skin color. It's got everything to do with your motivation. You may think we've coddled her, and maybe we have, but she's my princess, and she deserves to be treated as such. A man simply making ends meet won't do."

I was wrong. His words weren't a punch to the gut but rather a knife that plunged deep into my belly. My face flushed with embarrassment. I blurted the first thing that came to mind.

"I love her, Lonnie."

He patted my knee. "Sometimes, that's not enough."

Lonnie stood then and left me sitting on the front porch. The door locked behind me.

Chapter 21

Tina cocked her head. "Is it true?"

We were seated in the visitor's lobby again—the counter with the plexiglass between us.

"About Mike?" I nodded.

She appeared sad, but not the weeping heartbreak I might have expected.

"What happened? Butch didn't tell me much except he was dead."

"Squirrel and Bumps gunned him down."

"Those two? They didn't even know him."

"Squirrel knew him. Mike and he fought."

"Because he was trying to help me?"

I shrugged. "I think so."

She gnawed on her lip. "Could Squirrel and Bumps have killed Carlton?"

"It doesn't make sense."

"Does killing Mike make sense?"

"In their world, you bet it does. Mike beat up Squirrel. Eye for an eye. Killing Carlton doesn't have any type of payoff. At least, it doesn't seem that way."

She whispered, "My husband and my ex-husband." The words were filled with regret, and her gaze drifted off to somewhere over my shoulder. In a moment, she muttered, "I feel bad." She sounded confused.

"Tina, are you okay?"

She blinked, and her gaze returned to me. "I'm fine."

"Are you sure?"

A small, apologetic smile crossed her lips. "I'm not

going to hurt myself if that's what you're worried about."

"I wasn't."

"I feel bad about Mike. I know he loved me, but I didn't love him that way anymore. And I swear to you, John, I didn't give him any hope that we'd ever get back together."

"I know."

"But that wouldn't stop him."

"I know that, too."

"So, I feel bad he was killed, but not like I'm going to die because he's gone. Does that make sense?"

It did. There were those in our lives whose deaths would rip a hole in our existence. There were others whose deaths would simply be notations in a journal. It surprised me that neither man warranted a bigger response.

Tina continued. "I also feel bad about Carlton. Even though—" She touched the side of her face. "A divorce was coming. Whether I was comfortable or not, it was coming. He was changing, and I couldn't keep doing what I was doing. But I miss him in sort of a hollow way. Do you understand?"

Her eyes darted about as she thought. "He seemed moody as of late. Like nothing was making him happy. We hardly had sex anymore, and when we did…" She lowered her eyes. "It was all about power. Games to get him excited."

"Did he hurt you during those moments?"

"Not really. It was just humiliating more than anything. For whatever reason, I think that's what he wanted to do to me." Sadness passed over her face. "I guess what I'm dwelling on is that Jaime doesn't have a father anymore—real or step." Her gaze drifted away from me and into a distance far away from the moment. "Shouldn't I have broken down by now? Shouldn't I feel like the loneliest woman in the world?"

"Maybe you will."

"What if I don't?"

"Worry about it tomorrow."

She nodded. "What are you going to do now?"

"Find Squirrel and Bumps."

***

I drove slowly through the parking lot of the gray apartment buildings. Only a few people wandered to or from their cars. On my initial pass-through, I didn't see a black Escalade. That didn't mean there couldn't be one in the neighborhood. Perhaps, they parked it a block away and trotted home. I zigzagged around the nearby areas— no Escalades of any color.

And from what Tina told me, Carlton had purchased two Escalades for his friends. So, at any moment, Grouch and Bone could show up.

Some of me wondered if the Dead Boys would be at Hoopfest today, but I realized that would be stupid. The cops wanted Squirrel and Bumps, and one of the first places they'd keep an eye on would be the basketball tournament. The crew had to know that.

The other would be the apartment community. I told Detective Ackerman where the Dead Boys resided. I didn't hold anything back. There was no need to do such a thing.

Maybe I should leave it alone, but Tina was still in jail, and I believed in her innocence. Just because Squirrel and Bumps killed Mike wouldn't zero out the Coeur d'Alene cops' belief that Tina had murdered Carlton.

I returned to the apartment community and took another

pass through the lot—still no Escalades or marked police vehicles. I backed my truck into a spot that gave me a view of the Dead Boys' apartments.

Scanning the parking lot again, I searched for people sitting inside a vehicle. If this had been a long stakeout, perhaps the cops could have used an apartment across the way to keep an eye on the crew, but time was short. They'd have to do it the way I was. Either someone would be in a vehicle, or maybe they'd pretend to be grounds workers or some other type of outdoor laborer. It was Sunday, and no one was out maintaining the lawn.

Fifteen minutes passed, and nothing caught my attention. Why wasn't an officer posted here? Had they already apprehended the Dead Boys and were now questioning them? Or had Ackerman and the Spokane Police Department not notified their cross-border brethren? I found the second possibility hard to believe. Maybe the first occurred.

Or perhaps a patrol unit had been here surveilling the apartments, and an incident happened that required them to leave. That I *could* believe. Which meant I only had a small window of time to move as I'd already wasted more than fifteen minutes driving through the neighborhood looking for black Escalades and then surveilling the lot.

Reaching for the glove box to retrieve my gun, I paused. I wasn't licensed to carry in the state. If I was sure that the Dead Boys weren't in their apartments, I didn't need a gun. And if I believed a cop was in the parking lot, then I shouldn't get out of my truck. In Washington State, burglarizing a dwelling while possessing a firearm was a Class A felony. I didn't know what that equated to in Idaho, but it couldn't be good.

I left the gun where it was, but I did pull out a pair of

leather gloves. I did occasional things for a friend that the law would have frowned upon. Fingerprints and witnesses were things I had to consider—just like now.

On the landing for B326 and B327, I tried the knobs on both doors. Locked. Then I knocked on B326 and waited. Nothing. Same thing with B327. Knock and no response.

Eeny meeny. I kicked in the door of B326. The jamb splintered as the door burst open. Before I could catch it, the door bounced off the back wall. Just in case someone rushed with a gun from a backroom, I hesitated to enter. When no one appeared, I stepped inside and closed the door. It wouldn't secure.

I hurried through the apartment, looking for anything that might be of help. In the kitchen, I found a day planner filled with contacts, addresses, and phone numbers. I grabbed it.

In the living room were a bong and a small bag of marijuana.

Clothes were strewn about the floor of the first bedroom. The smell of man hung in the room.

The second bedroom didn't reveal anything more than the first. It was cleaner, and several books were on the nightstand near the bed, but I didn't find anything of evidentiary value.

I left the apartment and pulled the door closed. It still wouldn't latch completely.

Clutching the day planner, I knocked again on B327 and moved to the edge of the landing to see if anyone was walking nearby. When I was a kid, we would say the coast was clear when making a mad dash for something. I hadn't said that in probably twenty-five years, but that silly saying came to mind.

I stepped back and booted the door to B327. It popped

open with less enthusiasm than the first apartment. I stepped in, noticed splintering along the jamb, and closed the door. This one, too, failed to properly secure.

The living room was clean, but I found a half-empty box of .40 rounds in the kitchen.

The first bedroom was basic. Nothing hung on the walls. There was no television anywhere. An opened suitcase was on the floor of the closet. Neatly folded clothes were inside.

In the second bedroom, framed prints of sunny beaches decorated the walls. I checked underneath the bed. A digital camera was on the nightstand.

It took me a few seconds to figure out the device, but the camera beeped and came to life when I did. I selected review mode and saw a few posed pictures of the Hispanic woman. This must be Bump's.

None of the photographs were nude, and many seemed to have artistic quality. I looked at the framed pictures of the beaches. Had Bumps taken those, too? Was he an amateur photographer?

Time was running out for me to be in the apartment. I'd already committed a felony by being here. Taking the camera wasn't going to make it much worse.

As I left, I pulled the front door shut behind me.

Chapter 22

I set the day planner and the digital camera inside my desk at my office. The thirty-minute drive home hadn't calmed my nerves nor settled the ethical demons waging war inside my heart.

Burglarizing the Dead Boys' apartments was easy. Now, I had to live with the guilt. Most shitty things I did rarely bothered me at the moment. It was the lingering remorse that did me in.

I walked Corporal to the park. It was mid-afternoon, and the sun scorched. I unclipped his leash and sent the big dog running after the scruffy tennis ball. We only played the game for a few minutes before he dropped near me. His tongue drooped from the side of his mouth.

We spent a few minutes running through his commands, but he didn't seem motivated for the drills, and my head wasn't into it either.

Back home, I stood in front of the oscillating fan with my arms spread wide. The dog sat on the floor watching me.

"We should get air-conditioning," I said.

With a groan, Corporal flopped to his side.

"Yeah, yeah, I hear you."

I sat at the desk and removed the organizer and the camera.

Inside the day planner were various plastic cards to Blockbuster, Starbucks, and Sprint. However, there were actual credit cards. Several business cards were stuck inside the front pouch. Two of them were for attorneys out of Southern California, and one of them was for a car detailing business in Post Falls, Idaho. The calendar was blank except for a few noted birthdays.

The phone list was filled with initials and addresses out of Southern California. I slowly flipped through the alphabet until I found a location in Spokane. The initials K.H. lived in the East Central neighborhood. I wrote the address in my notebook and put the organizer to the side.

Next, I checked the camera. Bump's photographs of the Hispanic woman showed his talent. He'd taken some of her at Hoopfest. Several others had her in a variety of outfits. It appeared that she dressed up so Bumps could photograph her at a lake, on a train trestle, and in a darkened alley.

The pictures of the Hispanic woman stopped and were replaced by photos he'd taken of the Dead Boys and Carlton Winfrey at a party. They were of the same artistic quality, though. Rarely did anyone look into the camera. And when they did, it wasn't in the amateurish way that most of my photographs came out.

Had the guys become accustomed to having Bumps around with a camera? Or did he delete the photographs he didn't like and keep only the good ones? Whatever it was, the pictures that remained from the party were as good as those that came before.

The Dead Boys and Carlton Winfrey looked natural as if he'd caught them off guard, but not in the silly ways others did when they got ahold of a camera. These were careful photographs, and the pictures made everyone appear natural.

The first photograph that I paused on was Carlton Winfrey sitting on the edge of a couch. It seemed like the one at the second apartment. Winfrey was bent over with his elbows at the knees. He appeared pensive with a cigar in his hand. Worried, maybe. It was an excellent snapshot. If Winfrey was a more prominent name, Bumps could have sold it to a magazine like *Sports Illustrated*. Hell, maybe he still could.

The following picture showed Bone whispering into the ear of a white woman. Her head was kicked back, and she was laughing. It was clear she enjoyed whatever he was saying.

Next, Squirrel stared directly into the camera but was clouded by a poof of thick, white smoke. The following photograph was of Squirrel again but from a different angle. This time, a joint dangled from his lips. He seemed older than his natural years implied.

I leaned in to study a picture of Grouch. He seemed to be animatedly talking to the Hispanic woman and her black friend. However, that wasn't what interested me. The motion in the back of the photograph caught my eye. Carlton Winfrey appeared to be carrying a woman in a blue dress down the hall.

I flipped back to the picture of the woman Bone was talking to. She wore a yellow blouse and white slacks.

Now, I was on a mission. Who was Carlton Winfrey carrying?

It took almost a dozen pictures until I found her. She never got to be in her own photograph. Had Bumps tried, and she forbade it? Was that because she was aware of Bumps walking around with a camera? Or was Bumps successful in taking her photo and later deleting it?

In the background of one photograph of the Hispanic woman stood Olivia Wagner in a blue dress. With both hands, she clutched a red plastic cup. She appeared apprehensive—the classic wallflower. Or was it because she knew her fiancé would disapprove of her being there?

Why was she there?

The party's artistic photos soon ran out and were replaced by more pictures of the Hispanic woman and her poses.

I returned to the beginning of the party photographs but moved through them carefully this time. No attention was paid to the photographer's skill. Instead, I looked for the blue dress.

In all those photos, Olivia Wagner appeared only twice—once when she stood as a wallflower in the background of another's photograph and the other when Carlton Winfrey carried her down the hall.

Chapter 23

The drive back to Coeur d'Alene seemed faster than usual, probably because I spent most of it worrying.

I thought about calling the local police and having them meet me there. I didn't, though. I'd have to explain how I came into possession of the camera. If two wrongs don't make a right, what do two felonies make? Probably five to ten. Burglary isn't looked upon very highly, no matter how good my intentions were for committing the crime.

Olivia Wagner met me at the door. "Mr. Cutler?"

"Can I come in?"

Her eyes narrowed. "For?"

I lifted the camera and showed her a picture. "You lied."

She stared at the camera for a moment, then stepped back. The door opened as she did so. We took up our previous positions—her in the chair, me on the couch.

I asked, "Is your mother home?"

"She's in the back—gardening."

The time for being gentle was over. I needed to get to the truth. "You lied about not going to their parties."

Tears welled in her eyes, and her chin dimpled as she tried to contain her emotions.

"Whose apartment was the party at?"

"LaShaun's."

So, Bone and Bumps were roommates, I thought. "Why'd you finally agree to go?"

Olivia shrugged. "My friend, Greta. She wanted to go."

"How did Greta find out about the parties?"

"I told her."

"How did you find out?"

"Carlton's friends invited me. They said the invitation was from him—that he liked the way I looked." She squinted at the memory.

"Did Carlton ever invite you?"

"Once when he saw me walking through the neighborhood. When I said no, he asked me out."

"Carlton asked you on a date?"

She nodded. "I thought it brazen, too. His wife and daughter were in our neighborhood. I think they were home when he did it."

"If you weren't neighbors, would you have gone?"

"I'm engaged, and he was married. Certainly not."

"Did you tell anyone?"

"Besides Greta? My mother."

That's why Kay seemed surprised when her daughter denied knowing Carlton the other day.

"What did they say about his advances?"

"My mother told me to keep it to myself. She's all about appearances. Greta told me I should go out with him or at least go to a party."

I leaned forward. "Why would Greta give that advice?"

"She hates my fiancé and wants me to dump him. There's bad blood between them. Scott wants me to stop being friends with her, too. I feel caught in the middle."

"Why'd you agree to go to the party?"

"Greta. She kept pushing me to go, so I finally agreed for her."

"No offense, but that seems a flimsy reason to go."

She lowered her eyes as her hands rubbed together. "Have you ever been unhappy? Like really unhappy— almost dead inside?" She touched her sternum. "You want to find an answer but don't know where to look. It's not about hurt or pain. It's about nothing. It's about a hole. Scott thinks the problem is inside my head. My mother blames my father's passing. Me, I think it's because I'm supposed to do something else with my life."

"And you went to that party for an answer?"

She shrugged. "People do drugs for an answer. They hurt themselves because of that hole. Going with Greta was a convenient excuse to step outside of the safe little box my life had become."

On the camera, I flipped to the photo of the woman laughing with Bone. "Is this Greta?"

"That's a nice picture." She turned away.

"What happened when you arrived?"

Olivia shrugged. "The party was already going. JayJay and Oscar had dates. Real pretty girls. Sort of crass, but nice. They didn't like me too much, but they took to Greta. She fit in quickly. Supposedly, some other girls were supposed to be on the way. Carlton came over and started talking. Said he was happy that I was there. We chatted about nothing really, just everyday nonsense. What restaurants we liked. What our favorites movies were."

I nodded.

"He said he liked me, which I thought was weird because he didn't even know me. He said I was beautiful. That I should be treated like a queen. He asked if I would go out with him after the party. I reminded him that he was married and that I was engaged. He laughed it off. Said he was getting a divorce, so he was essentially already single. I told him I had to go, but Greta was having too much fun. She was getting a lot of attention from Oscar."

I didn't see any pictures of Greta with Grouch. Only the one with her laughing with Bone.

"When I asked her to leave, Greta begged me to stay. She was my ride so—"

"You could have called your mom or your fiancé."

Her face hardened. "I could never call Scott."

"I've met him. I understand why."

Olivia looked at the floor. "Scott's views are— they're not mine, but they're sort of tolerated around here. The first time he expressed them, I was surprised. Not that he voiced them, but that I wasn't offended. I worried that it made me a bad person." She rubbed her forehead. "I mean, if I love a man who has those views, does that make them my views, too? Am I making sense?"

"You are."

"You're polite. Anyway, that's why Greta hates Scott. She knows how he feels about people of color and gay people and, well, anyone that's different. But there's more to him than that." She looked away. "When he doesn't talk about that stuff, he's a wonderful person."

I'm not sure what Olivia Wagner could see in Scott Fairchild, but there were plenty of times when I questioned what a woman saw in a man or vice versa. It wasn't about that bullshit of the heart wanting what the heart wanted. It was about humans sacrificing their standards or morals to avoid feeling alone.

I flipped through the photos on the camera. When I found what I wanted, I held up the screen. "In the background of this photo. What happened?"

She leaned forward to study the picture, and her features flattened. Her hand covered her mouth, and she looked away.

"Olivia?"

She stood and moved behind the couch. It took a moment for her to compose herself. When she did, she said, "Greta wanted to stay, so we did. Carlton brought me a drink. He made a big show of apologizing." Her smile was full of regret. "He'd become very charming and promised to be on his best behavior for the rest of the night." A shiver ran up her body. "I should never have had that drink."

I set the camera next to me and watched her deal with her demons.

"My body felt as if it moved away from me." She looked up. "That's not right. My consciousness moved away from my body. I could sense it happening to it but couldn't control anything. I couldn't fight back. I was helpless. Carlton picked me up and carried me into one of the bedrooms."

"What did everyone else do?"

"Nothing. The ones that were there carried on like it was the most normal thing in the world."

"Who was there?"

"Only JayJay and his girlfriend."

"Where was Greta?"

Olivia eyed me. "She wouldn't want me to say."

"Listen. I'm not judging anyone. Suppose Greta hooked up with LaShaun or Oscar then more power to her. I'm trying to understand where everyone was in relation to you and Carlton."

"Greta went with LaShaun and Oscar to the other apartment."

I quickly did the math.

Bone and Grouch took Greta back to the other apartment.

Bumps and the Hispanic girl were in the apartment when Carlton raped Olivia. It probably occurred in Bone's room.

I asked, "Where was Squirrel—Andre? Where was his girlfriend?"

"He'd left to take her home."

"Why didn't you report it to the police?"

"And tell them what?"

"The truth."

"And have my fiancé find out? And have the world know what Greta did?"

"Greta's a grown woman."

"No," Olivia said. "I made my decision."

"Did you tell Greta?"

She shook her head. "I was gone before she woke up."

"How did you get home?"

Olivia straightened and crossed her arms. Her brow creased as if she were in deep thought.

"Someone took you home, and it wasn't Carlton. If you don't tell me, I will be forced to reveal this to Tina Winfrey's attorney. He'll reveal the information to the police who will—"

"LaShaun. LaShaun brought me home."

I cocked my head.

"When Carlton finished, he left me there. He walked away from me like a piece of garbage. I floated in that room for what seemed like an eternity. There were voices in the room next to me."

Bumps and the Hispanic woman, I thought.

"At some point, I fell asleep. I woke when LaShaun shook my shoulder. He seemed so tall. I thought he might hurt me, but he spoke to me in a reassuring tone. He put my dress back on. The whole time he cooed to me like I was an injured bird."

"Olivia, did you see Tina's car outside the Winfrey house the morning Carlton was murdered?"

It appeared that she had difficulty swallowing before the tears started.

"Olivia, what kind of car did you see that morning? Was it an Escalade?"

Her eyes flashed away.

"Who was there that morning? Was it Bone? Was it LaShaun?"

Olivia stood. "It's time for you to go."

"The statement you gave the police put an innocent woman in jail."

"You need to go."

"Olivia, please—"

"You heard her, Mr. Cutler," a woman's voice came from behind me. Kay Wagner stood in the entryway. "It's time for you to go."

The elder Wagner walked over to her daughter and hugged her. Olivia buried her head in the nape of her mother's neck.

"Now, Mr. Cutler," Kay said.

I let myself out.

***

As soon as I left Olivia Wagner's neighborhood, I pulled to the side of the road and thought.

I could call Butch Hollingshead and tell him about Olivia's lie. He would likely notify the police, who in turn would reinterview Olivia.

Maybe she'd admit to the lie. Maybe she would admit to Winfrey's rape. Her fiancé, Scott Fairchild, would find out. God knows why she loved him.

I flipped open my notebook and considered the East Central address for the unknown K.H. It was the only

Spokane address I'd found in the organizer I'd taken from one of the Dead Boys' apartments. That was another lead I could follow.

Perhaps it would lead me to Bone, and I could ask him about that night. Or maybe it would lead me to Squirrel and Grouch—the guys who killed Mike.

Finding K.H. seemed the best course of action.

***

It was easy to find the East Central address. It was a single-family home set several lots in from the corner of Fourth and Helena. I passed through the neighborhood searching for black Escalades. Not finding any, I parked and observed the house.

A concerning thought hit me then—the Dead Boys might have changed rigs. The black Escalade was an easily identifiable vehicle. Maybe they dumped them somewhere and switched out to something less conspicuous. Perhaps they had a local connection who hooked them up with a non-descript grocery-getter.

Great. Now, every vehicle was suspect.

If I was afraid to ring a doorbell, I should call Tina's attorney now and let the cops deal with it. Of course, I would have to explain how I possessed some knowledge, which might reveal that I committed two burglaries.

It felt wiser to play this lead out.

No one answered the doorbell. After a minute, I knocked.

A mid-forties black woman opened the door. She was attractive but not in the way Carissa Taylor was. It was a working woman's beauty. Her hair was short, and her eyes revealed the years. She wore blue jeans and a gray t-shirt.

Soapsuds covered the long latex gloves she wore. "Can I help you?"

"Is K here?"

"Krishawna?"

"Yes, ma'am."

Her eyes flicked to the lock on the flimsy screen door. She reached out and secured it. "What's this about?"

"A friend of Carlton Winfrey's."

"The man that was murdered?"

I nodded.

"Why would—" Her lips pursed. "This is about Squirrel."

"Yes, ma'am."

She took a moment to take me in. "You're a cop."

"Private investigator." I pulled out my wallet and removed my license. Her eyes narrowed as she leaned into the screen door to study it.

"John Cutler," she said.

"Yes, ma'am."

"I guess you want to know my name."

"Only if you want to tell me."

Her eyes registered suspicion.

"It would be helpful, ma'am, but I'm okay if—"

"Robin Hayes."

K.H., I thought. Krishawna Hayes.

Robin crossed her arms. "What's he done?"

"He and his friends were involved in a shooting."

"Did someone die?"

I nodded.

"And you think Krissy was involved?"

"I don't know, ma'am. Andre was—"

"Squirrel," she interrupted. Her lip curled. "She insists on calling him that."

"Squirrel was with a young woman last night and—"

"Where?"

"At Club Royale."

Her face hardened. "You saw her?"

"The young woman? Yes, ma'am, but I don't know—"

"Wait here." She stalked away.

From inside the house, I noticed a lavender aroma. At least, I thought it was lavender. Whatever it was, it smelled lovely. A moment later, the woman returned without her rubber gloves. She held up a framed photograph to the screen door. It was a high school senior's portrait. "Is this her?"

It was the woman I'd seen with Squirrel at Hoopfest and in the line at Club Royale.

I nodded. "That's her."

She pulled the photograph back and stared at it. Her hands tightened around the edge of the frame.

"She might not have done anything, ma'am."

The woman looked up.

"Krissy was at the Club before the shooting. I don't know if she was in the car when they did the drive-by."

"I told her to stay the hell away from that boy and his friends. That this sort of thing would happen."

She was working herself up, which wasn't going to help me.

"Robin, I don't want to bother your daughter—"

"Better you than the cops."

"But I need to find Squirrel. When will Krissy be home?"

She flicked a hand. "Who knows? But if you want to talk with her, she's working at that Starbucks over on Sharp. The one near the Gonzaga campus. She gets off at six today."

I pulled out a business card and stuck it in the metal edge of the screen door. "In case I miss her. Please ask her to call."

"If you find him, will you arrest him?"

"I'm not the police, ma'am."

"Then what are you going to do?"

"Ask some questions."

"Well, don't be afraid to smack him around." She frowned as she closed the door.

Chapter 24

If Krishawna Hayes worked until six, I had some time to run a personal errand.

Erika's Honda was no longer parked in the driveway. Maybe she moved it inside the garage. Rather than stop and risk a possible confrontation with Carissa and Lonnie, I continued to my house. Her car wasn't there either.

I hadn't expected it, but childish hopes still get the best of me now and then. This was one of those times. Erika hadn't returned a half-dozen calls nor a couple of clumsy texts. If she wouldn't respond, I'd have to find her.

After refilling the dog's water bowl, I went downtown.

Hoopfest Sundays are much quieter than Saturdays. Most teams have been bounced from the tournament, and many fans don't come for the second day. I parked at the edge of the competition and walked toward Club Royale. The bar wouldn't be open yet, but I wanted to see if Erika might be there working.

As I turned the corner, I was surprised to see the hoops along this area alive with activity. I thought for sure the cops would have kept this area locked down for the day. A homicide had occurred here twelve hours ago. Had the department's brass made sure everything was cleaned up and gone before the first teams returned to play? Gang violence would not be the type of thing a city would want associated with one of its major sporting events.

Club Royale was locked. I tried to peek in through the darkened windows.

"They don't open 'til late," a woman said. She wore a

purple Phoenix Suns jersey and denim shorts that were frayed at the edges. Her face and shoulders were sunburnt.

The crowd behind us cheered something.

"But if you want," the woman said, "you can go to Mootsy's. They're open now." She pointed down the street. "The one with the yellow door."

"Thanks."

She held out her hand. "That'll be a dollar."

"For?"

"I just gave you directions."

"I didn't ask."

"But I gave them."

The woman yelled vulgarities as I walked away.

Fighting my way through the Hoopfest crowd was much easier today. I walked all the way east to Eight Ball Billiards. I didn't expect Erika to be here, but I felt lonely and wanted to speak with a friend.

As soon as I entered, I noticed a spike in customers. Most days, the place was barely full. Today, every seat was taken, and every table had a game going—except the one in the back corner.

A heavy-set man sat on the bench with his knees spread wide. In his fist, a pool cue stood upright. He looked like a poolhall version of King Conan. Disheveled hair, polyester slacks, and thick suspenders might not be the vision of a ruler, but if anyone needed information, Deacon was the man. I'd known him for a year now and still hadn't learned his last name. I doubt many people knew it.

As I approached, his eyes shifted to me. "John Cutler, you're overdressed for this day."

I sat next to him. "How's business?"

"The bar is doing fine."

"And you?"

A young couple came over to the pool table nearest us. The fresh-faced man set his hand on the rail and asked, "Is anyone on this table?"

Deacon eyed the younger man. I remained silent.

"Well?"

A tall man with broad shoulders and no neck came over. "The table is occupied."

The fresh-faced man looked up. "But nobody's playing."

"Yes, they are," Broad Shoulders said.

The young woman sidled up to her man. "This place is so rude. We're never coming back."

Broad Shoulders spread his arms wide to indicate the two only had one path, and that was toward the front of the bar.

When the couple left, Broad Shoulders returned to his place in the darkness.

Deacon shook his head then turned to me. "Are you working?"

"I am."

"What's it about?"

He intently listened while I spoke. As I finished, he pulled his handkerchief from his pocket and wiped his forehead. "So, what do you need from me?"

"Nothing."

He rolled his lips downward. "You come down here—" he waggled the pool stick in the direction of the other customers, "—with all these citizens just to tell a story. And you don't want to trade help?"

"I wanted to talk with a friend."

Deacon smirked. "Your friends end up murdered. I'd rather be an associate."

"Mike Davoli wasn't my friend."

"He was your friend. Maybe not now, but at one time."

"If you want to get technical."

"And that bothers you?"

I shrugged. "I guess I'm fine with it."

"If you were, you wouldn't say he wasn't your friend."

I watched a game of pool several tables away.

"No one is ever the same," Deacon said. "From day to day, everyone changes. Even you."

My gaze returned to him.

"Big events change us. Small events, too. It could even be something we read. Do you read?"

"I do."

"What's the last thing you read that affected you?"

I thought about Crumley's *The Last Good Kiss*. "I'll probably mess it up."

He waggled his cue. "Give it a go."

"'Life begins and ends in a bloody muddle.'"

"That's not so bad."

I shrugged. There was more to it. How life is one big mess from womb to tomb, and we're left to rot in the sun like a can of worms. Crumley did it far more justice than I could have, so I left it alone. Deacon seemed mollified anyway.

He eyed me. "So, this friend drove a wedge between you and your girl?"

"Erika."

"What're you doing about it?"

"Not much I can do. She won't return my calls. I can't find her. And even if I do, she probably won't listen to me."

"You've already explained the situation?"

"Repeatedly."

"Have you listened to her?"

"I have."

"Without the expectation of countering back?"

I frowned.

"Sticks and stones break bones, John, but words kill love. They kill trust. You need to listen to her without being defensive. Without trying to explain anything to her."

***

The parking lot of Starbucks was full, so I parked on Mission Avenue. Inside the coffee shop, an unoffensive jazz song played. All the tables were filled with customers—most seemed preoccupied with books or newspapers.

Behind the counter was the woman I'd seen with Squirrel. She saw me and smiled. "What can I get started for you?"

"Coffee. Medium."

Her nametag confirmed that she was indeed Krissy. She tapped a few buttons on the register. "A Grande Pike. Anything else?"

"That'll do it."

I handed her a five, and she made change. Without any further chatter, she turned around and filled a cup. Giving it to me, Krishawna Hayes said, "Have a nice day."

"You, too."

I walked outside.

***

Fifteen after the hour, Krissy strolled outside and across

the parking lot. Seeing her, I headed in her direction.

"Krissy," I called.

She stopped and eyed me. "Black coffee, right?"

I lifted my cup.

"Listen, I don't go out with older guys."

"What about Squirrel?"

Her eyes narrowed. "Older *white* guys."

"That's not what I'm after."

Krissy's face hardened. "I don't know any Squirrel."

"Yeah, you do."

"Who are you?"

"My name's John Cutler. I'm a private investigator."

She smirked. "Investigating what?"

"A drive-by shooting at Club Royale."

"When did it happen?"

"Last night."

Her eyes narrowed with surprise. "For real?"

"You were there with Squirrel."

"It must have happened after we left."

"Why'd you leave?"

"That line was total bullshit." She waved her hand. "It was taking forever. We were never going to get in."

"Where'd you go after?"

"I don't have to tell you."

"No, you don't."

She turned and headed for a white Honda CRX.

"Hey, Krissy."

"What?"

"I'll let the cops know where they can find you."

She faced me. "Cops? Why'n the fuck would they want to talk with me?"

I moved closer to her. "They're going to want to know what you know, but they won't be as respectful as me, though. I waited for your shift to end."

"I don't know nothing about nothing."

"You know Squirrel and Bumps. Where'd you go after you left Club Royale last night?"

"Nowhere."

"Save your story for the cops." I turned.

"Wait!"

I stopped.

"Gabby and me, we—"

"Gabby? Is that the Hispanic girl with Bumps?"

Krissy nodded.

"Gabby, what?"

"Hernandez. Gabriela. The boys told us to go down to the Big Easy and wait for them. They said they had to pick up Bone and Grouch at Crazy 8's."

"Did they do that?"

"I guess so, but they never showed at the Big E. We couldn't get in because of their line. Waste of a perfectly good night." She disgustedly shook her head.

"What'd you do?"

"Gabby and I rolled with it."

A police car drove southbound on Hamilton. "Where is Squirrel now?"

"I'm not telling you that."

"Because he's your man?"

"My man?" She appraised me. "The seventies called. They want you back."

"Okay, don't tell me about Squirrel. Tell me where I can find Bone."

"How would I know?" Krissy clucked her tongue. "And if I did know, I sure as hell wouldn't tell you. You're over your head, Sherlock. If you want to sic the cops on me, do it. I've got more important things to do than stand around talking to you." She clapped twice. "See ya."

She dropped into the CRX. I moved out of the way as it reversed from its parking stall. The car zoomed out of the lot and into traffic.

***

I called Erika again, but it went straight to voice mail. I didn't leave a message.

***

The west end of South Hill is known as Cannon Hill. Small apartment buildings are sprinkled among ornate, turn-of-the-century homes. Spokane's older neighborhoods were notorious for this economic schizophrenia.

Marian Howell lived in a brick house with a nicely manicured lawn. Elm trees shrouded it with shade. The front door was open. Behind a wood-framed screen door, the front door was opened. Carol King's "I Feel the Earth Move" played somewhere inside.

The screen door bounced as my knuckles rapped against it.

A head popped around the corner. "Hello?"

"Hey, Marian. It's me."

"John. Hold on."

She disappeared into the room. When she came back into full view, she wiped her hands with a cloth as she approached the door. Marian wore denim overalls covered with paint splotches. Her salt and pepper hair was long and wiry. She lifted a hook off the screen door.

"Come in, come in. Let me wash my hands."

I followed her into the kitchen.

"Can I get you something?" She put her hands under the faucet. "Coffee or a glass of water? I'd offer you a beer, but I don't drink."

"No, thanks."

She turned off the faucet, then flicked the water from her hands.

"How was your trip?"

"Fine, I guess. I haven't processed it yet. Spreading ashes is supposed to be cathartic. At least, that's what I read, but she was my mother. I loved her probably more than anyone. It still feels weird to be without her."

I didn't comment. The relationship with my mother was strained. I'd dealt with the guilt of being a bad son most of my adult life. When society says a boy is supposed to revere his mother but doesn't, it leaves him feeling as if he's broken in some way.

Marian dried her hands then faced me. She looked tired. More than the first time I'd met her. I pulled out the ring from my pocket and handed it to her.

When she opened it, tears welled in her eyes. "Thank you," she whispered. The box snapped closed, and she clutched it to her chest.

"You're welcome."

"Were there any problems in getting it?"

I shrugged.

"I'm sorry."

"Part of the job."

"Did he…" Her voice trailed off. "Who gave you the ring?"

"She did."

Marian studied me. "Were you uncomfortable?"

I thought about Terry punching me in the parking lot.

"Not really."

"Most men are. Some women, too. I'm sorry. I shouldn't have asked. It's none of my business."

"It's okay. It's his life. His journey. You helped me understand that in our first meeting."

Her smile was polite. "Thank you for saying that. Some of our friends are mad at me for ending it." She rolled the box in her hand. "They say I should have been more understanding, but Terry was an angry person, and they didn't see it. I saw it. We only show our true selves to those closest to us. I was afraid when he got angry. He'd get out of control."

I thought of Terry. She seemed to be in control of her anger. There were only a few flashes of it, and even when we fought, she seemed to have it in control. Maybe that was the fighter's discipline.

"You're thinking about something," Marian said.

"Terry. I can't see her as out of control."

"She wasn't. He *was*. I'm not a psychologist, but I think it has to do with how he felt. When he's her, it feels natural and okay. The anger subsides. When he's him, it's there." Marian's face pinched. "I'm not trying to make it sound like a mental condition." She tapped her chest. "Terry can't be who he is, who she is until they decide one way or the other. Does that make sense?"

"I think so."

She stared at the box in her hands. "When she was happy, I loved her. When he was happy, I loved him. But he was rarely happy. His anger was scary, and I didn't want to be around that."

"You don't have to convince me."

Marian looked up. "Our friends have picked sides. It's a terrible place to be."

"I understand."

She moved to a counter and grabbed a checkbook. "How much do I owe you?"

Chapter 25

Major Crimes Detective Gary Ackerman dropped by my house the following day. He knocked on the door and waited.

I was in the park with the dog. I threw the ball again and sent Corporal after it.

The sun seemed extra cruel that morning, and the air had a heaviness to it. That didn't stop activity in the park, though. The pool was already filled with kids, and the basketball courts were alive with pick-up games.

Ackerman checked his watch, then looked toward the community center. He knocked again but didn't bother to wait. Instead, he returned to his car.

I hollered, "Ackerman!" Yelling detective in my neighborhood wasn't a good idea. About as bright as yelling 'cop' or 'narc.'

Ackerman searched for the origin of his name, saw me, and waved.

I threw the ball again, and the dog went after it. Corporal's enthusiasm had a short shelf life even at this time of the morning. We'd been out here twenty minutes, and the sun had zapped him. If I wore a full-length fur coat while sprinting after a ball, I'd probably be worn out, too.

The detective headed toward a bench in the shade and sat. When Corporal returned, I joined Ackerman. The dog lay next to me.

"That dog freaks me out."

"That's his job."

"Still."

"Is there a reason you're throwing off the vibe of my neighborhood?"

"Oscar Greene's been arrested."

"Grouch? What for?"

He watched as a couple of women in shorts and sports bras ran by. When they passed, Ackerman said, "I think I went to high school with the one in the red." He turned to me. "An ISP trooper stopped him in Coeur d'Alene Saturday night—before the shooting."

I ignored his question. "What'd they stop him for?"

"Crossing the white line."

"He was intoxicated?"

"Not drunk, but yeah. Marijuana. They took a blood sample. He's on parole, so the DUI stop was a violation. ISP contacted his parole officer, who violated him. Greene is being extradited back to California."

"So, he was out of the mix for the drive-by. Anything on the others?"

Ackerman shook his head. "No, but we think something's going on with them."

"How so?"

"After Saturday's shooting, we contacted the Coeur d'Alene Police Department and alerted them to Murphy and Robinson. Asked them to keep an eye on their apartments."

I didn't like where this story was headed. Scratching Corporal behind the ears allowed me to avert my gaze.

Ackerman continued. "They were short-staffed, so they couldn't put a unit on the apartments full time. They were doing the occasional drive-by. Just a knock and check sort of thing. Yesterday, they found both apartments broken into. That allowed them to conduct a welfare check."

"Did they find anything?" I had to ask something—

remaining silent would look suspicious.

"On the initial search, they found some drug paraphernalia and ammunition. Based upon our information and their welfare check, they secured the apartments and got a couple of search warrants."

"And?"

Ackerman shrugged. "Nothing."

"What is Coeur d'Alene PD doing now?"

"They'll write up some chippy arrest warrants for the paraphernalia, but I doubt they'll go anywhere. The real mystery is how the apartments were broken into."

I scratched the dog's head some more.

"Any ideas?"

"Maybe the Dead Boys pissed off the wrong guy."

"You think one guy did this?"

"It was a figure of speech."

"Huh." The detective watched the two women jog by again. "Nope. Too young. Didn't go to high school with her."

"You came over to my house to tell me this?"

Ackerman stood. "Yup."

"Why?"

"It's a nice morning, and I wanted to get out of the office."

I stood, and the dog jumped to my side. The three of us crossed the street.

Ackerman stopped at his car. "Hey, John."

After stepping onto the sidewalk, I turned around.

"If you know anything, tell me. Okay?"

What I knew now would lead back to the felonies I committed in Coeur d'Alene. At this point, I needed to keep the information about Krishawna Hayes to myself until I could turn it over to Butch Hollingshead. "I don't know anything."

"In that case, stay out of trouble."

Ackerman slipped into his car and started the engine.

***

I drove by Krishawna Hayes's home and didn't see her there. The tiny house didn't have an attached garage, so I looped around the house to make sure her car wasn't parked in the back.

Next, I continued over to the coffee shop. Her car was in the lot, and I took a spot across the street. She hadn't seen my truck, so I wasn't worried about it being spotted.

I wasn't sure when her shift ended, so I settled in for the day. I'd brought along a bottle of water and two peanut butter and jelly sandwiches. It was best not to drink too much lest I have to hit the head. If this was night, I could always pee in a bottle and not worry about leaving my vantage point. However, relieving myself inside my truck during broad daylight was not advisable. There were too many things that could go wrong.

Slightly after two, Krissy walked out toward the white CRX. The little car zipped onto Mission Avenue. She sped by me as she headed eastbound. I pulled into traffic and did my best to keep a safe distance behind her, which was harder than it sounded.

The woman drove like a maniac. She weaved in and out of traffic as if she were racing for a checkered flag. A driver of a rusted pick-up angrily shook his fist after she cut him off. He was still yelling when I passed him.

A BMW full of teenage boys pulled up next to her. The two cars raced north on Division, and I had to blow a red light to keep Krissy in sight. Eventually, a clump of traffic slowed both vehicles, and I caught up.

Krissy's head bounced to some thumping music. I heard it when I got near.

The CRX zipped into North Town Mall's parking lot. She found a parking spot near the entrance. I circled the lot as she trotted inside. If she spotted me following her, there was nothing I could do. However, I had to believe she didn't.

I looped the lot in hopes of finding a spot that would allow me to spy on her vehicle. Eventually, I tired of circling and waited in the No Parking zone.

A couple of minutes later, mall security arrived in a small sedan. They activated their emergency lights which called additional attention to my position. I abandoned that post and circled the lot again.

Twenty minutes later, a parking spot opened, which allowed an unobstructed view of Krishawna's car. I still had one sandwich left, so I ate it.

Krissy soon walked confidently out of the mall. In her left hand was a small, pink shopping bag. It swung as she moved.

The CRX chirped when it left its parking stall, then zoomed out of the parking lot. Northbound traffic was thick, but she zipped in and out of it like it was a video game.

My truck sat up high so I could see her when she got into the distance. I thought I was about to lose her when she pulled into the left turn lane. Southbound traffic slowed her from entering the business she wanted.

I couldn't pull in behind her and risk revealing myself, so I drove on by. As I did so, she whipped into the parking lot of the Spokane Motel. I quickly lost sight of her car.

It took a minute to turn around and make it back to the

motel. My truck slowly crept around the building. Krishawna entered a room just as I cleared the building.

In front of the room was a black Escalade.

***

The Spokane Motel is the kind of single-story facility that cropped up in the mid-part of the twentieth century when automobile travel still seemed romantic. Now, it's relegated to those travelers with too little money or those hoping for a low profile.

Its white paint job had yellowed and flaked in large chunks on the southern side. The parking lot had alligatored, and several sections had potholed. Even with those warts, the motel's parking lot was full. And it wasn't cheap vehicles either. Besides the Escalade, there was a newer Lexus and a well-maintained vintage BMW.

I backed my truck into a spot, so I could watch the room that Krishawna had entered. I turned off the engine. In less than a minute, Bumps and the Hispanic woman walked out. He held the door to the SUV open for her. Bumps laughed as she passed by. She must have said something funny.

What was her name? I reached for my notebook but stopped when I remembered it. Gabby Hernandez.

Bumps walked around to the driver's side, and the black SUV left the parking lot.

Krishawna and Squirrel were now alone in the room. I could go and knock on the door, but I didn't need that kind of hassle. I'd found Mike's shooter. It was time to call in the cavalry.

I called Butch Hollingshead. His assistant patched me through.

"John?"

"I've found Andre Murphy and JayJay Robinson."

"Call the police."

"I might have gotten the information that led me to this point under questionable methods."

Butch sighed. "So, you need me to alert them?"

"If you don't mind. Call Detective Ackerman of the Spokane PD. He's working Mike's murder."

"This is blurring our relationship."

"I understand."

He sighed. "Give me the address."

We finished our conversation and hung up.

There was nothing to do now but wait. I turned on the radio. Britney Spears' "Toxic" started, and I had to turn it down. My fingers drummed on the steering wheel, and my head bobbed along with the rhythm. I'd heard the song often in the club and knew the words.

Maybe I should leave, I thought. There was no reason to hang around. If the cops were coming, they would contact Squirrel. I put my hand on the ignition key and was about to start the engine when the door to the hotel room opened.

Squirrel walked into the parking lot and turned around to wait for Krishawna. He exhaled a plume of cigarette smoke. He hollered something I couldn't hear over the music.

I turned Britney off.

Krissy Hayes appeared now and pulled the door closed behind her. The two started across the parking lot. They didn't seem as happy as Bumps and Gabby were. They walked in step with each other.

My gun was still in the glove box. I froze with one hand on the wheel and the other on the ignition. Making a move now would call more attention to myself.

Squirrel said something as they passed by my truck. Krissy looked at Squirrel and stopped when she noticed me behind the wheel.

She pointed and said something. Squirrel turned and saw me.

I made a decision then. More flies with honey. I opened my door.

Squirrel jerked up his shirt and pulled out a gun.

"Wait—" I hollered, but it was too late.

His gun boomed, and the window in the door exploded. I ducked and ran toward the back of the truck. Moving to the opposite side of the vehicle, I peeked around the corner.

Across the parking lot, the door to the hotel room closed. Squirrel and Krissy had run back into the room.

There wouldn't be much time before they realized that returning there was a bad move. I only had a moment to seize that leverage. I collected my gun from the glove box.

Curtains in the room opened slightly then dropped into place. I ran in a wide arc toward the hotel room. My shoulder collided with the wall next to the door. I didn't need to go in. I only needed to keep them there until the police arrived.

But I hadn't talked with Ackerman. I'd asked Butch to leave him a message. My phone was still in the truck. I didn't dare risk running back for it.

"Squirrel," I yelled.

A gun fired, and a bullet ripped through the center of the door.

From inside, Krissy shrieked. "What are you doing?"

"Shut it!" Squirrel shouted.

"Squirrel, don't shoot."

"I'm not going back to jail," he hollered.

From down the way, a shirtless man stepped out from his room. Using my thumb and pinkie finger, I mimed a telephone. He stepped back into his room as if he didn't want any trouble.

"Squirrel, put down your gun," I shouted.

"I'm not going back to jail!"

A low, rumbling engine entered the parking lot. As the black Escalade came around the corner, I could see Bumps behind the wheel. His eyes widened with recognition. The SUV accelerated. I dove out of the way before the vehicle slammed into the building.

I righted myself and came up with my gun trained on Bumps. The woman was no longer in the vehicle.

From inside the room, Krissy screamed. The Escalade had punched a hole into the room.

It appeared that Bumps was trying to put the vehicle into reverse but fighting with an exploded airbag as he did so.

Sirens were in the distance now. The cavalry was on the way. Butch's call must have made it through. Or perhaps it was the shirtless man from down the hall.

Bumps turned to see me with my gun. He frantically searched for something. He bent out of sight. I backed further away until I rounded the corner and lost sight of the Escalade.

When a patrol car burst into the parking lot, I dropped to a knee and set my gun on the ground. I lifted both hands.

From the opposite end of the parking lot, a second patrol car entered with its lights and sirens activated.

It sounded as if more engines roared into the parking lot.

"Drop the gun," someone yelled. "Don't do it!"

Several gunshots erupted.

I dove for the ground.

A moment later, someone dropped their weight across my shoulders.

"Stop resisting," a male voice ordered as my hands were roughly cuffed behind my back.

Chapter 26

The interview room's fluorescent bulbs hummed, casting the room in a bright white light accompanied by its own monotonous soundtrack. I laid my arms on the small table and rested my chin on the back of my hands.

After a patrol officer detained me at the motel, he sat me in the back of his patrol car. I was there for an hour in direct sunlight and without air-conditioning. I'm sure it wasn't intentional, but it would have been an effective interrogation tool had it been. I was softened for my pending interview.

A heavy-set detective arrived at the scene, peered into the patrol car window, and then directed the officer to take me to the station. I'd been sitting in the interview room alone for thirty minutes now. But this was a cakewalk compared to being behind the shield. I had legroom and air conditioning. I wasn't complaining.

There was no window in the room, though. I didn't bother to get up and check to see if the door was locked. I didn't care. Someone would talk with me sooner or later. I preferred it would be now.

The burly detective from the motel stepped inside. In his right hand, he carried a file folder.

From where I sat, he appeared six feet. He might have been taller, but the hunch he developed from carrying that much weight made him appear shorter. He wore black slacks and a wrinkled blue shirt. He had pasty skin, and his nose looked red and gnarled. On his hip, a Glock rested inside a leather paddle holster. His belly partially obscured the silver badge on his belt.

He cleared his throat and produced a thick, crackling sound. "I'm Detective Scarborough. You can call me Rollie." He sighed when he sat. "Helluva day, isn't it?"

Scarborough plopped the folder onto the table. He reached over to the wall and flicked a switch. Then he pointed up to a red light in the wall. "See that? We're being recorded." He flipped open the folder and removed a white card. "One of the uniforms Mirandized you at the motel, but I'm gonna do it again."

"You don't need—"

Scarborough interrupted. "You have the right to remain silent. Anything you say can and will be used against you in a court of law." He continued reading from the card until he finished, then he tucked the card into the folder. "Do you understand these rights as I have read them?"

"Is Detective Ackerman working?"

Scarborough frowned. "Did you not hear my question?"

"My attorney called Ackerman—"

"Your attorney?" His face soured. "Are you asking for an attorney?"

"No, I was wondering—"

He leaned over the table. "Because if I have to end this interview so you can talk with an attorney, that's going to make me real suspicious."

"I just wanted to know if Ackerman was working."

"So, no attorney?"

I shook my head.

Scarborough straightened. "Ackerman's around," he said absently.

"Can I talk with him?"

He read from the file. "Says here you're a private investigator."

I crossed my arms.

"How long you been doing that?"

When I didn't answer, Scarborough pursed his lips. "Is that how it's gonna be?"

"You want to talk. Okay, but let me say hi to Ackerman first."

"Ackerman's not going to get you any rhythm."

"Do I look like a dancer?"

Scarborough grunted and flicked off the video recorder. Then he stood. "Stay put."

"Where am I gonna go?"

***

Ten minutes later, Detective Gary Ackerman walked in. He didn't have a suit jacket on, but he looked sharp in his shirt and tie. He sat across from me. "Making friends, I see."

"Scarborough?"

Ackerman nodded. "Rollie doesn't like you."

"How's a fat bastard like that make Major Crimes?"

"He was skinny when he started."

"Probably a ball of fire, too."

Ackerman wagged a cautionary finger. "Don't underestimate him."

"Did you get my message?"

"Through your attorney? Not much good it did. By the time he called, two men were dead."

"I figured Bumps, but no one has told me anything."

The detective shifted in his chair and crossed one leg over the other. "It's a mess from what I've heard. I haven't been up to the scene. Robinson came out with a gun, and the officers on scene dropped him."

"Why would he do that?"

Ackerman shrugged. "How would I know? You were there. Did he do anything?"

"He was looking for a gun when the cops arrived. At least, I think he was."

"Sounds like he found one. Maybe he was hopped up on adrenaline and wasn't thinking straight when he tried to exit the vehicle."

It bothered me that JayJay Robinson was killed. The man was talented. He had an artist's eye, but I couldn't reveal that to the detective without providing a link back to the crimes I'd committed.

Ackerman must have seen the disappointment on my face. "Life isn't like the movies, John. We don't always get to know the why."

"I know that."

"Things go from bad to worse in the blink of an eye. They rarely go from bad to good that fast."

I liked Ackerman, but I didn't need a lecture on human behavior. "What happened to Squirrel?"

"Andre Murphy? Robinson drove his car into the building—"

"He tried to squash me like a bug."

"Murphy was on the other side of the wall. Killed instantly."

I lowered my eyes. Squirrel's death didn't affect me. I held him responsible for Mike Davoli's murder. Mike had assaulted him, so he seemed the natural to want retribution. Maybe Bumps had pulled the trigger in the drive-by, but I wanted to pretend he hadn't. The pictures he took bothered me. A talent wasted, it seemed. But maybe Bumps didn't see it that way. Maybe photography was nothing but a hobby—a simple diversion.

"You okay?" Ackerman asked.

"Is the woman saying anything?"

"Sounds like she's playing it straight."

"That's good. What about me? Can you handle my interview?"

Ackerman smirked. "You know I can't do that. This is Rollie's case. Just tell him the truth and don't bullshit him. If he smells a lie, he'll bury you with it."

"Why would I lie?"

"He might look like a schlep, but he's a first-rate investigator." Ackerman stood. "You're lucky everything turned out okay."

"I think Bumps and Squirrel would disagree."

"I suppose they would."

He opened the door and vanished.

***

When Scarborough returned, the interview restarted as if it were never interrupted. The detective sat, flipped open his file, and said, "So, you're a private investigator?"

"That's right."

"Is that what you were doing up there at the motel? Investigating?"

I nodded. "I'm working for Butch Hollingshead. He's a defense attorney in Coeur d'Alene."

Scarborough's brow furrowed. "What case are you working on?"

"The murder of Carlton Winfrey. His wife was arrested."

"You're representing the wife?"

Another nod.

"And those guys at the hotel are tied into it?"

"They were friends of Mr. Winfrey."

Scarborough made a note.

"Childhood friends," I clarified.

"Ackerman seems to think Andre Murphy was the Club Royale shooter."

I nodded.

"Did you tell him that?"

"I did."

He looked up from his paperwork. The interview went easier after that.

Chapter 27

The sun was down when I made it home. I hadn't expected her to be there, but her car was out front. Erika sat on the steps, and the front door was closed. She wore a white t-shirt and black jeans. She shifted to the side as I settled next to her.

"Hey," I said.

Across the street, shadowy figures moved in the park.

"Want to go inside?" I asked.

"Sorry I haven't called. Had some thinking to do."

"I understand."

"What did you do today?"

I told her about the day's events.

"You saw two men die?"

"I was around the corner."

"That truck hit the building next to you, though."

"The guy was inside. I didn't see what happened to him."

She looked down at her feet.

"So, you figured out who killed Carlton?"

"Not yet."

"Two men are dead and—"

"Three."

She cast a sideways glance.

"Mike."

Erika looked away. "How could he be your friend?"

"People change."

"Not like that."

"I don't know what to say."

"That's what I was afraid of." She stood.

"Wait. That's all you came here for?"

"Pretty much." Erika walked toward her car. She stopped at the edge of the sidewalk and looked back. "You're not even going to try and stop me?"

I lifted my hands. "I don't even know what's going on here."

"Never mind."

She climbed into her car. It slowly left the neighborhood.

Chapter 28

I woke early and returned to Coeur d'Alene.

From my vantage point in the parking lot, I could watch the apartments owned by the Dead Boys. Oscar Greene was still in jail for a DUI and parole violation. Andre Murphy and JayJay Robinson were dead. Only one was missing.

I'd already checked the apartments. The door jambs had been repaired, and I would imagine that the locks had been replaced.

It was probably a waste of time to be sitting here, but I'd meet with Butch Hollingshead in an hour or so.

My life felt in shambles. My relationship with Erika was over. The only case I actively had was Tina Winfrey's. At this point, I wasn't even sure I wanted to practice as a private investigator anymore. Lonnie Taylor's accusation about me being an underachiever still cut deep.

I'd made a couple of toasted peanut butter and jelly sandwiches. I ate the first one and sipped some lukewarm coffee.

A hooded figure came around the corner. By the size and build, I knew who it was.

He passed by the stairwell to the Dead Boys' apartments but soon stopped and headed back. He was probably checking for patrol cars. An older F-150 doesn't scream law enforcement.

The figure climbed the stairwell. From where I sat, I couldn't see which apartment he entered.

I probably should have called the police, especially

since my gun was sitting somewhere in a Spokane PD evidence locker. Even though I hadn't fired it, the cops needed to confirm it. That would take time. I could have gotten one illegally, but I didn't think I'd need it. Maybe I was wrong.

It wasn't hard to determine which apartment he entered. The door was kicked in. Some poor maintenance guy would have a hard time fixing the jamb now. I knocked and pushed the door open.

He didn't appear.

"Hey, Bone," I called. "It's John Cutler. The guy you met in Riverfront Park."

His voice came from one of the bedrooms. "What do you want?"

"To talk."

He appeared then. His right hand was held behind his back. I knew what was back there.

"I'm unarmed," I said.

"Are you alone?"

"Yeah."

He walked into the kitchen and set his gun on the counter. "So talk."

"I want to know what happened to Carlton."

Bone crossed his arms. "Why should I answer your questions?"

"Because I'm trying to get Tina out."

He cocked his head. "Krissy called last night. Were you the motherfucker who was there when Squirrel and Bumps got it?"

I nodded. "But I didn't kill them."

He put his hand on top of the gun. "How did it happen?"

"Bumps tried to hit me with his car. He hit Squirrel instead."

Bone closed his eyes. "Mother fuck."

"Then the cops showed up and Bumps—"

He lifted a hand to stop me. "Those two—" He didn't finish that thought. "Goddamn it. They had to go and shoot the ex-husband. Then Grouch disappeared. I haven't heard shit from him."

"He got snagged by state patrol for a DUI. They contacted his parole officer who violated him."

Bone rolled his eyes. "We should never have come up here." He sounded sad.

"You came for Carlton."

"We should have told him no." He put his hands on the edge of the counter and leaned over the gun. "Hell, we should have told him to stay away from us down in LA, too. Coming back to the scene changed him."

"Changed him how?"

Bone looked up.

"When he left the neighborhood, he was a good kid. Maybe a little naïve, but he was going places. We all knew that. He had natural ability. You got to be special to play college ball."

"Sounds like Carlton had his head on straight."

Bone shrugged. "Mostly. He couldn't get into too much in Tacoma or Utah, but when he came home..."

"What happened?"

"Us. He started hanging with us again and doing things he never did when he was younger. I beat the shit out of Grouch for hooking him up."

"The majors test for drugs, right?"

Bone shook his head. "Carlton wasn't using, but he was acting like Dr. Feelgood. Giving shit to girls he met."

"Like a dealer?"

"Some took it willingly."

"He drugged them?"

Bone pushed off the counter. "It was a weird game to him. I think he liked it better if the girl wouldn't participate. Then he'd get to slip her something and take it by force."

"The other guys knew?"

"He was the center of the party. What were they going to say?"

"And Tina?"

"He should never have married her. She didn't deserve what he was doing."

"I thought you didn't like her."

He eyed me.

"You *did* like her."

"Not like that, but it doesn't matter."

"What happened to Carlton?"

Bone looked away. "There was this girl back home— Monique. Real nice. From around the way. Seventeen. Smart. Going somewhere. I was in love with her sister, but she wouldn't give me any play. Monique came to one of our parties. Carlton showed up and took a liking to her, but she didn't dig him. Too old. Too married.

"Carlton liked them that way—cold. Really charged him up. I asked him to leave her alone because of her sister, but he told me she would be his. He dropped a tab in her drink. It didn't take long for them to end up in a bedroom. When he was done with her, he let some of the guys run a train."

"Squirrel and Bumps?"

Bone waved a hand. "Nah. Grouch neither. Just some of the other dudes at the party. When no one else wanted a piece, Carlton wanted the crew to drop her someplace where she could find some more action. The thought of it made me mad, so I told him I'd take care of it. I put the girl in my car and drove her home. The entire way back, she stared at me with tears streaming out of her eyes. I picked her up and put her on the front porch of her house. I knew there was no way Monique's sister would ever talk to me after that.

"Back at the party, people laughed about it. Even the girls thought the shit was funny. People put up with a lot when there is free booze and drugs, and Carlton made sure everyone was cared for. Monique never told anyone, and I never stood against what happened. Four days later, she killed herself. Took a bottle of painkillers and never woke up."

"And then it happened again," I said. "With his neighbor."

Bone shook his head. "Stupid fucker."

"You hooked up with her friend while it happened."

He seemed offended. "I didn't know he would pull that shit up here."

I lifted my hands in deference.

"The woman was a freak, but Olivia was a citizen and square as they come. Carlton had to see it, but he still went through with it. It's like he wanted to get burned by the fire. When I took her home, all I could think about was Monique and how she killed herself. After I left, I kept thinking, was Olivia next?"

Bone's face hardened. "I don't have a problem with killing a man, but rape—" His eyes darkened. "I should have stopped Carlton long ago. What he did to Olivia was on me."

"How'd you know to go over at that time of the morning?"

His laugh was without joy. "Tina thought she was sly,

but she wasn't any good at sneaking around. I found out about her boyfriend before we ever came up here. That goofy, long-haired bastard. She snuck over to see him at the weirdest hours. Was doing that back home, too."

"Why didn't you tell on her?"

He looked at me as if I were stupid. "I just told you what her husband was doing. The woman had a right to get some on the side."

"But you punched me when I mentioned it in the park."

"Yeah? Well, appearances had to be maintained."

"So, you what? Let yourself into the house, found a knife, and put an end to it?"

He leaned against the counter. "It was quick. Quicker than what he did to those women."

"But then Tina was arrested for it."

"I thought I'd get in and out without anyone seeing me."

"Olivia saw you that morning and lied because you tipped the scales of justice for her. Now, an innocent woman is sitting in jail."

"I didn't expect Tina to go to jail for it, but then she had to go and lie." Bone put his hand on the gun. "But if you expect me to go quietly with the cops. That ain't gonna happen."

"Relax," I said. "I've got a way out of this. For you, Olivia, and Tina."

He cast a sideways glance.

I laid out my plan. When I finished, I asked, "Will Grouch be a problem?"

He shook his head. "He'll play his part."

"Then it's time you call the cops. I'll get rid of that gun."

Reluctantly, he grabbed the firearm by the barrel and handed it to me.

Chapter 29

The six o'clock news started, and I asked the bartender to change the channel and turn up the sound. A group of businessmen briefly eyed me with contempt but turned their attention to the barkeep's butt when she extended her hand for the volume control.

The evening's top story was the latest break in the Carlton Winfrey murder. A reporter standing outside the Kootenai County courthouse said, *"In a stunning development, the main witness in the Carlton Winfrey murder recanted her story today. The charges against Tina Winfrey have been dropped, and she's being released."*

The face of Coeur d'Alene Police Chief Sanborn popped onto the screen. He scowled while he spoke. *"Our witness changed her statement for reasons we can't verify at this time. Due to this new information, the prosecuting attorney has decided to drop the charges against Mrs. Winfrey."*

"Who is your main suspect now?" a reporter asked.

The chief stared directly into the camera. *"The main suspect in the murder is JayJay Robinson. Yesterday afternoon, Mr. Robinson was killed in a shootout with officers of the Spokane Police Department."*

Some of the guys around the bar grumbled that they wanted to watch some sports. The bartender eyed me. Sports sounded great.

After our talk, Bone called the police, and I went to Olivia Wagner's house.

It took some convincing, but I suggested she change her

statement. At first, she was reluctant to believe me, but I assured her this would protect LaShaun. She cried then.

We practiced what she would tell the police. She would recant her original story and say she saw JayJay Robinson the morning of the murder. However, she was afraid to tell the truth because Bumps and Squirrel had threatened her.

Judging by the news report, she did just fine.

I'm not sure what Bone would say to Grouch to get him to fall into line. Maybe nothing. Maybe Grouch would know to stay the course.

I finished my beer, dropped some bills on the bar, and headed home.

Chapter 30

The phone woke me. The clock showed it was a few minutes after eight. I'd gotten almost eleven hours of sleep.

When I answered, I mumbled, "Hello?" My voice was froggy.

"John? This is Butch Hollingshead. Are you still asleep?"

"Not anymore."

"I assume you've heard the news."

"Yeah." I rolled onto my back.

"Draft an invoice and send it over. Let's get you paid."

The grogginess dropped away. "Okay."

"Get up, John. There's a whole day waiting for you."

Before I could come up with a snarky reply, Butch clicked off.

***

After a shower, I cleaned the house, then threw the ball with the dog in the park. When we returned home, I made a list of attorneys to call to drum up some business. Even though I was second-guessing private investigation as a career path, I didn't have any other job prospects. Bouncing at the club and seeing Erika right now didn't sound appealing.

I called her several times but finally gave up by early afternoon. I thought about dialing her parents but knew that would end in disaster. If Erika didn't want to see me,

I didn't need Lonnie or Carissa to deliver the bad news a second time.

I was nursing a beer in the backyard when the doorbell rang.

It wasn't the woman I was hoping to see.

"So, this is where you live?" Tina Winfrey said. She wore a summer dress and flip-flops. Her hair and make-up hid the fact that she spent the last week in jail. "Can I come in?"

I stepped back. "What are you doing here?"

"I came by to say thank you."

"You're welcome."

"Have you anything to drink?"

"Beer. There might be a bottle of merlot somewhere."

"Let's go with the wine."

She sat at the kitchen table while I opened the bottle. "This is a change from where you used to live."

"You should have seen my previous apartment."

"Small?"

I popped the cork. "Something like that." I poured two glasses and handed her one.

She clinked hers against mine. "To freedom."

We sipped our respective drinks.

Tina looked over the lip of her glass. "Bone called after I was released."

"What did he say?"

"That he was sorry for how things turned out."

"That's nice of him."

She considered the wine. "Unlike him but nice."

"People change."

"Some do."

"What are you going to do now?"

Tina sipped some wine. "Head to my mom's and get

Jaime."

"Then?"

She shrugged. "I don't know. I don't want to go back to California. Maybe I'll go back to Seattle. I liked living there." She rolled her glass between her hands. "Maybe I could pick someplace new and start over. Somewhere no one knew me or my past."

"Running away doesn't make it disappear."

Tina raised an eyebrow. "That sounds like experience talking."

"It is."

"I'm sorry for dragging you into this."

"You didn't. Mike did."

She smiled. "But you helped me."

"We were friends."

"We still are."

I touched my glass to hers. "To old friends."

She shared my toast and then ran a finger around the edge of her glass.

"When are you leaving?" I asked.

"Tomorrow. I've got my bags in my car. Movers are scheduled to pack up the house next week. They can do it without me."

"Where are you staying tonight?"

"Downtown. I've booked a room. I'll get an early start in the morning."

"Sounds like you've got a plan."

She stood and slipped her hand into mine. I tightened when she leaned in to kiss me, but her lips landed on my cheek.

"Thank you," she said. "I'll never forget what you've done."

She touched my face before leaving. I waited until her

car left the neighborhood. Then I went out back and sat on the steps. Corporal lumbered across the yard. He put his head on my lap and looked up at me.

"You're a good boy," I said.

I wondered if he thought I was a good man.

Did You Enjoy the Book?

Thank you for reading *Cutler's Friend*. I'm always grateful when a reader takes time out of their day to comment on one of my novels. If you do write a review, please email me and let me know. I'd love to say thanks!

About the Author

Colin Conway is the creator of the 509 Crime Stories, a series of novels set in Eastern Washington with revolving lead characters. They are standalone tales and can be read in any order.

He also created the Cozy Up series which pushes the envelope of the cozy genre. Libby Klein, author of the Poppy McAllister series, says *Cozy Up to Death* is "Not your grandma's cozy."

Colin co-authored the Charlie-316 series. The first novel in the series, *Charlie-316*, is a political/crime thriller that has been described as "riveting and compulsively readable," "the real deal," and "the ultimate ride-along."

He served in the U.S. Army and later was an officer of the Spokane Police Department. He's owned a laundromat, invested in a bar, and run a karate school. Besides writing crime fiction, he is a commercial real estate broker.

Colin lives with his beautiful girlfriend, three wonderful children, and a codependent Vizsla that rules their world.